# THE
# BEAUTY

## ALIYA
## WHITELEY

**TITAN** BOOKS

The Beauty
Print edition ISBN: 9781785655746
E-book edition ISBN: 9781785655753

Published by Titan Books
A division of Titan Publishing Group Ltd.
144 Southwark Street, London SE1 0UP

First Titan edition: January 2018
10 9 8 7 6 5 4 3 2 1

Edited by Anne Zanoni & George Sandison.

This is a work of fiction. All of the characters, organizations,
and events portrayed in this novel are either products of the
author's imagination or are used fictitiously.

A CIP catalogue record for this title is available
from the British Library.

Printed and bound in the United States.

For H.C.M.W.
who proves that change is possible

# PART
# ONE

To start—

There are signs, I don't care what William says. There are signs of change, of regeneration, and I saw the first mushrooms in the graveyard on the morning after I ripped up the photograph of my mother's face and threw the pieces over the cliff, into the fat swallowing folds of the sea.

Timing is everything.

My name is Nathan, just twenty-three and given to the curation of stories. I listen, retain, then polish and release them over the fire at night, when the others hush and lean forward in their desire to hear of the past. They crave romance, particularly when autumn sets in and cold nights await them, and so I speak of Alice, and Bethany, and Sarah, and Val, and other dead women who all once had lustrous hair and never a bad word on their plump lips. I can remember this is not how they were; I knew them, I knew them! Only six years have passed and yet I mythologize them as if it is six thousand. I am not culpable. Language is changing, like the earth, like the sea. We live in lonely, fateful flux, outnumbered and outgrown.

Last night I spoke of Miriam. She was the teacher with a passion inside her, always burning hot, making her ferocious. When the inspectors would climb up through the rocks from the town and tell her it was their right to judge her lessons, she would fling pieces of paper at them, plans and registers, and she would sneer, a skewed expression of her natural superiority. Then, after the inspectors roared away, she would rip the papers to pieces, make celebratory confetti and tell us to dance in it.

Miriam once caught me trying to make my own records of attendance like I had seen, all our names, ticks and crosses, marks and meanings. She threatened to hold my hand over the fire if I didn't destroy it. She said nothing good comes from anything but natural rhythms: daybreak and sunset, spring and winter. So we learned to read storms in the laying down of cows and when to plant pumpkins in the wake of runner beans. Those were our lessons, until our strengths had been discovered, and then we were given our tasks.

Miriam died early, one of the first, with the yellow fungus thick on her nose and tongue. It crawled out from her womb and down her legs.

I did not speak of death. I painted her in words of sweet sepia. She once held the hands of the little ones during lambing, cherishing the placentas, the blood of renewal. I spoke of that, and the others nodded as if they understood what she was.

Today the world moves on, and I must find new ways to turn the truth into stories. The graveyard bears more mushrooms, clustering in soft wet shapes, yellow folds and rivulets, in the outlines of the women beneath the soil. It must mean something good. William must be made to see it.

\* \* \*

'It means nothing,' says William.

He isn't our leader. We don't have leaders. But he is the person who gives advice that everyone listens to. I once asked Miriam what word we could give to him that would explain that—maybe a new one, made from our minds? She threatened to chop my brain into bits and feed it to the chickens for being so cheeky. I still don't understand why.

Such thoughts about language cannot be scooped from brains anyway. This is why I say things I shouldn't.

'Can I at least name them?' I ask William.

He stares into his stew, in the earthenware bowl. It is a hearty lunch, good in the autumn days when the sun gives only a weak warmth. Thomas is always generous in his portions, perhaps because he likes the taste of his own cooking so much, unlike Diana, who always made measly meals and ate not at all.

William says, 'Why do these mushrooms need a name?'

I say, 'For stories?'

'You're going to tell a story about toadstools and fungus?' William heaves his shoulders, like the bulging of a laugh that can't escape his stiff belly. 'I might skip the fireside tonight, then.'

'They are growing from the bodies of women.'

'That's true, Nate, but that doesn't make it important.'

'Are we not important, then? We grew that way too.'

William puts down his spoon, his thoughts written in the line of his lips. 'You are the strangest lad,' he muses. 'I don't want to hear tales of growth and bodies. Talk about the beginnings of the Group tonight; I like that story the best.'

A long sigh escapes me before I can swallow it. It doesn't go undetected by William's ears. He gives me a look of pity, and says, 'Tell you what, take Thomas with you and he can see if there's eating on these mushrooms.'

'They're not that kind—'

'Nate,' he says, and the conversation is closed. I leave him to the remnants of his carrots and the tough sheep stew, and tiptoe away before he can change his mind.

\* \* \*

William was once married. He lived out in the world, a city-crawler, like an insect. Marriage was a piece of paper and on it you wrote your name and the name of the woman, like paper could be a stone to the mouth of a cave and you could both be sealed within. As time moved around, a work of constant motion, William came to see that the paper meant nothing, and the city was only a swirling mess of life within which he had become lost.

So he left his wife and pointed himself south-west, ending up by the sea, in the Valley of the Rocks, where a small Group of like minds had made a place. And he found he fitted there.

When he told me about his journey, that was how he finished it—he fitted there. I find this to be the strangest of expressions—how does one fit in to other people, all edges erased, making a seamless life from the sharp corners of discontent? I don't find anything that fits in such a way. Certainly not in nature. Nothing real is meant to tessellate like a triangle, top-bottom bottom-top. The sheep will never munch the grass in straight lines.

It's a puzzle which my mind keeps returning to, making it difficult to focus on Thomas's ramblings as we make our way to the graveyard. He talks of all the mushrooms he has found this autumn and the dishes he has made with them. Thomas is puffed up with his own importance as the cook, even though he is younger than me and no doubt thinks it is my duty to listen to him; but I am thinking of triangles all the way to the wooden crosses, where the shapes cancel each other out and leave me empty.

'There's no eating on them,' says Thomas. He's looking at the mushrooms: dense balls with gilled undersides, yellow with ragged browning edges, clustered on each mound of earth like flowers left for the dead. They have multiplied since yesterday. Some are as big as my fist. 'It's the colour. It's a warning, isn't it. Like red berries on green bushes. Don't eat us, it means.'

Even though I know he's right about the mushrooms, I say, 'We eat raspberries, though. And strawberries.'

He rolls his eyes, but takes a few steps towards Annalisa's grave. She was so young, just a new baby, born with the yellow disease stretched tight over her like a caul. Doctor Ben said he would have had to slice off her skin to save her. Such thoughts chase away raspberries in a flash.

Still, Thomas pulls his sleeve over his hand and picks a small one, then brings it to his nose and sniffs. He inclines his head, as if trying to decide if the wine is rancid, and a memory comes to me of another time, a night in my teenage years when I drank too much cider and giggled through the autumn festival until I nearly fell into the bonfire and my mother pulled me back to her arms and made me sit by her feet for the rest of the party.

To have someone who tells you what to do—sometimes this seems like a bad thing, and sometimes it doesn't. Is anything forever? I'm thinking not.

Thomas holds the mushroom to my nose, and says, 'Meaty...' I inhale, and, yes, there is the tang of meat on it, not unpleasant, like beef slow-cooked to softness. But when Thomas pokes out his tongue and holds the yellow ball to the tip of it he recoils, shudders, and says, 'Bitter, bitter.' We both know that is a sign of poison. He spits and says, 'No good can come of it.'

'You talk like an old woman,' I tell him, which is true, although I doubt he can remember how old women talked. They had a kind of bellicose gabble on them, gathering in groups like geese, all honk and no teeth. But Thomas is barely out of his teens and not popular with others his age. Maybe because of that impressive belly, or the fact he already has a job, a good one, while the rest of them are still under the care of Eamon, who took up teaching when Miriam failed.

'I do not,' says Thomas. 'Actually. Can you tell a story about my mother tonight?'

'Can't. William has asked for the story of the Group. Besides, I only spoke of her last week. She sang lullabies to you in the sweetest voice and knitted you blankets, don't you remember?'

'Yes, but I wouldn't mind more.'

I say, 'That's what they all say.' I am stretched thin with their wanting sometimes, but I wouldn't change that feeling of being needed, of being necessary. 'You can have a story about her soon,' I tell him. 'Can I have it?'

Thomas says, 'Wash your hands afterwards.' He is so very authoritative in his field; he likes his power, just as I like mine. Perhaps we two will lead the Group one day, in the final days. He adds, 'What are you going to do with it?'

'Take it to Doctor Ben, I reckon. It might have medicinal benefits. If they're springing from the bodies of women maybe they contain, I don't know, an antidote.'

'It's a bit late for that,' says Thomas, with a laugh, and I know for sure that he doesn't remember his mother, or any woman, to be able to wear that expression in this graveyard.

The disease that killed them all—it has become safe to him. He has never even considered the idea that it might grow, change, come for us men one day.

I know Doctor Ben has thought of this. He discussed it once with me, when I sat with him at dinner and collected the memories of his sister, who lived longer by scraping it out of herself with a knife for a while. He told me diseases are like people. They fight and fight and throw themselves around to escape the walls of tighter and tighter boxes.

In truth, if this happened it would only speed up the inevitable. There will be no more humanity after us; at least, none here in the Valley of the Rocks. Out there, beyond, there might be men in laboratories with tubes and eggs making fresh women, golem women as Doctor Ben says sometimes. It makes me picture white rooms with pink limbs, breasts and heads, pinned to long tables, the scientists in shiny coats taking them and building women one organ at a time. It gives me shuddery dreams.

I think if there were real women in the world I would have felt it, just like I feel spring's shoots arriving and winter creeping over the rocks. But there is only silence, only silence in the soil.

'You're right,' I tell Thomas. 'It's too late for that.'

Something in my expression stops his laughter. We look around the graveyard. The rough fence, chicken wire and wooden posts make a sorry sight. Some men put a pebble in front of the cross of their loved ones—wives, daughters, mothers—a count of pained days. Now these little stones make pyramids and spill over into the soil. They are interspersed with the yellow growths, making a pattern I can't interpret.

'What do you think Doctor Ben will do with them?' says

Thomas, as we leave the graveyard. 'Grind them into magic pills?'

'Take two in the morning after drinking new cider to cure your headache.'

'Take three and your cock will stop throbbing like a thumb hit with a hammer.'

'We're all saved!' I say, and this time we both laugh, facing the sea, feeling the freshness of the foamy waves crashing until it is difficult to remember what we are laughing for.

\* \* \*

Doctor Ben is the oldest of us. He came from just outside the valley with Teresa, his sister. Neither of them liked the outside world much, and he'd been coming into the Group to treat illnesses and injuries for a good few years before he made the decision to join. His sister said if he was going she was too. She was not a woman to be argued with.

I remember when the two of them came up through the valley with three suitcases of differing sizes between them, matching red and sleek with little wheels on the bottom. They struggled along with those cases as if they were more important than the journey itself.

Ben still has those cases. They sit in the corner of his house, unchanged and immutable. They continue to mean something to him, just as they mean something different to me. I never can take my eyes from them when I sit in his room.

The rain strikes the canvas over our heads with regularity, even jollity, as Ben throws mint leaves into mugs of hot water, which he collects from the fire. I stare at the suitcases and wonder what happens now in the world when people want to leave a place. There are still boats and aeroplanes, we see them; but there is no new place to go any more, no escape to be made on little shiny wheels.

He hands me my tea, then sits at his desk and looks at the fungus I have placed on it. He pushes it across the grainy wood with the blunt tip of his pencil.

'Where did you find it, Nate?' Ben asks.

'The graveyard.'

'And there are lots?'

'Getting bigger every day.'

'Every day? Visibly?' He shakes his head. Ben says, 'That's odd.'

'You think?'

The mint tea is refreshing and tingles on my lips. Doctor Ben puts his face close to the mushroom, eyeing it. He sits back on his stool. We don't talk for a while. The noise of the rain cheers me, makes me feel close to him; we are allies in this endeavour. Once before, he said to me, 'We are like minds, aren't we?'—and I agreed, all the time my mind elsewhere, flying over the peaks in the skies of my stories. But now I am here, all of me, content in his company and with my mug of mint tea.

'What will you be telling us about tonight?'

I say, 'The start of the Group again. William asked for it.'

'I'll look forward to that.' He swallows and says, 'Every time you tell it, it's better than the one before.'

I say, 'Thank you.' He looks surprised, and then I think that maybe he didn't mean it as a compliment. 'But it's always the same story.'

'Is it?'

Stories are as slippery as seasons; it's beyond my power to make either stand still. I try to tell them the same way, but each telling leads to small changes; something is added to the structure, a change of pace, a tweak of testimonies, all of them make circles in our minds.

Our friendship is broken once more. The rain has dried and the tea is gone; the yellow mushroom is shrivelling before our eyes, and the stalk is oozing a greyish gunk. Within a moment it is half the size it was and the liquid is sinking into the wood of the desk, making a smell like earthy compost.

'I think we should declare the graveyard off limits for now,' says Doctor Ben. 'I'll talk to William about it tonight. After your story.'

It doesn't need to be said that such a decision will not be popular. I am not the only one who will miss those quiet mounds, even though the men say: *I see Cathy in the stars, not at a graveside*, or *Sandra's body is not important. It never was, so it makes no difference where it lies.* They say these things reasonably with their logical heads while their hearts lead them to the graveyard to sit, to place their pebbles.

I don't place pebbles on my mother's grave. I look for meaning in the crosses. They are letters too; they form words, if only I could read them.

'Something is changing,' I tell Doctor Ben.

'Winter is coming and the mushrooms will die out in the cold.'

'For a while.'

'Sometimes,' says Ben, as he stands and stretches out his old muscles, 'you think too much.'

'Thank you,' I tell him again, and grin at him until he sighs and shoos me away.

\* \* \*

The windmill turns, the fire jumps high and the river tumbles over the stones. It grows dark and the wild goats bleat in chorus, giving their sad farewells to the sun.

I am ready. The men and boys have eyes only for me. I don't need to stand or wave my arms around. Attention is not held by the gimmick but in the kindness of my voice.

I tell the story of how we came to be.

*In the beginning there was the Valley of the Rocks. Huge stones lay amidst tough grass as if thrown from the sky by a giant hand, wild goats browsed and for a long time nobody came. The Valley waited for its purpose to be revealed to it. It watched the turn and tide of the sea and measured the months that turned to years, decades, centuries. It did not suffer from impatience. It held tight to its implacability, keeping itself intact: stones, grass, goats.*

*People came and went. Nobody settled the Valley. Nobody felt welcome. The soil was hard and unyielding and the goats were too fast to catch. There were better places to live around the Valley, with fertile fields and running water.*

*Eventually, when every other place had been built over and dug up, people returned to the Valley and named it a place of natural beauty, simply because they had not attempted to beautify it. The rocks and grasses and goats were photographed and post-carded, until the experts came and said:* These tourists are making the valley unstable. The Valley needs room and space and privacy if we are to keep it. *The Valley did not care. It could not be kept—it had not been owned to begin with.*

*Everyone was sent away, and the Valley waited.*
*Then we came.*
*The first of us: Tim, Mick, Bernie, Andrea, Pam and Polly.*

*They wanted to live a different kind of life, a better one. They moved into the Valley, and laid down the first tenets. Fresh air. Space for the kids. Growing our own food. Making our own goods. Getting electricity from the wind and water. Building homes out of mud and canvas. They fought a bitter war against the councilmen, but their struggle attracted others, like minds, and our Group swelled. The talents brought into the fold were many and varied: those good with paper, good with words, good with growing, good with building.*

And so on, like a fish in a river, I wind my way through the past. I am slick and shiny in the delight of the tale. It unites us, of course, but it also excites us. These stories of our fathers and mothers are a gift to the Group cut and polished with my words, and it leads to a wild night and the cracking open of many cider jars. The victory dance is done—we are still here. We beat our feet on the Valley that waited for us. Half of us lie in the forbidden graveyard, but the rest of us go on. For now.

And even without women there is still, once the cider is thick and mellow in stomachs, love. Tenderness. Maybe not for the older men who refuse such things, but the teenagers turn to each other and disappear into the darkness just beyond the boundary of the fire to play their games, and that is good.

But tonight I am spent. I swim on to the end of the tale, where it becomes the open mouth of the world into which all such stories pour and intermingle. I let it trickle away through my fingers with the words—and so it goes on.

The noises of love come in the wake of my voice and I look around those who are left alone. Doctor Ben is not to be seen; perhaps he has gone for an early night. He looked old this afternoon, too weary to face another winter. I am beginning to know that look. Thomas is not here either, and that makes me uneasy. Thomas never gets lucky with the other teenagers—he is more likely to be mocked than sucked—and he never misses the end of a story.

I catch William's eye across the fire and he frowns, pausing in his conversation with Hal and Gareth, the gardeners. I hear a cough close to my ear and turn my head to find Uncle Ted smiling at me, squatting to my level. It is a delight to see him at the campfire. Usually he keeps his distance, living wild like the goats. He brings logs and kindling every few days, and maybe rabbits or squirrels to eat.

Uncle Ted is always silent. Nobody ever hears him come or go and I can't remember the last time I heard his voice, so it is a wonderful surprise when he says, 'How are you, Nate? Good? All good?'

I pat him on the back. 'Yes, good. You're here, that's better than good.'

'Have you been to her grave today?' he asks me.

So that's why he's here. He is my family, my last remaining blood. He mourns his sister as I mourn my mother, different facets of the same woman. I know he visits sometimes; I saw the handfuls of forget-me-nots last spring. Our paths never cross there and I would not want them to. Grief is better alone. It has a cleaner taste, a sharper edge, that way.

I nod. I say, 'I've seen the mushrooms.'

'Can they be cleared away?'

'We don't know. I could try.'

'Don't touch them,' he says. 'They're not right. The animals stay away from them. They're in the woods as well. Perhaps they spring up wherever there's been a burial.'

'You mean a—body? Other women?'

He nods.

I ask, 'Why would they be buried in the woods?'

'I don't know.'

These unknown women, so close to us, faceless and erupting into yellow, bother me greatly. There is threat here, creeping towards our rocks. The mushrooms are not a good thing. They are not a beginning. I see in Uncle Ted's eyes the same knowledge. 'Thomas,' I say. 'Thomas and Doctor Ben. They touched the mushrooms.'

'Where are they now?'

'I don't know.'

He gets up and walks over to William. The two gardeners shrink back. He is a tall man, and a big one. My mother was the same—a large woman, muscled, respected. She was an engineer who made the windmills work and the houses strong enough to survive storms. I'm reminded of her in the way Ted moves.

William and Uncle Ted talk, their heads together, in the way that people with power do. Then William beckons me over.

'We'll need to find them,' he says, without pre-emption, and the hunt begins. We don't involve anyone else. I start at Doctor Ben's hut, find the empty sleeping bag on the pallet, then go to the communal hut to search for Thomas, stepping carefully around the lads in their ones and twos. He's not there.

So we raise the alarm. William rings the bell that hangs outside his hut—the sound is heavy, thickening the night with dread. Search parties are formed. As William directs matters, Uncle Ted whispers in my ear, 'Come with me,' and I do as I am told. We leave the fire behind, and the huts. We walk past the gardens and the graveyard, up into the rocks, then down into the woods leading away from the sea. Ted keeps a steady pace within the circle of his torchlight and never stumbles; I find tree roots rising up to meet my feet, tripping me and taunting me in the dark.

'Stay close,' he says.

Of course I have been in the woods at night before. Often in summer in my school years we would take our sleeping bags and head out. 'All the enemies had gone,' said Miriam, 'no boar, no bear, no wolf. If you see a pair of eyes in the night it's an owl,' she said. 'If you hear a noise it's a deer. Nobody ever got hurt by owls and deer, except mice and berries.' Are the woods still filled with the birds and beasts alone? Or are there new eyes, new creatures springing up in the gap left when the world had women ripped from it?

'Here,' Ted says. He stops and shines the torchlight on the bracken and blackberry bushes. I see mushrooms: squatting, swollen balloons with soft downy caps. They seem to squirm in the beam of the torch. 'It's gone.'

'What?'

He points. 'There was a large one. Shaped like a head.'

'A human head?'

There's no sign of it—no ragged stalk, no space on the ground where it might have grown. There's no point in asking him if he's sure we're in the right place. He knows the woods better than anyone. I have to trust his judgement. Part of me is glad this thing is gone, this head growing in the dark.

'Somebody must have taken it,' says Uncle Ted, and that thought is worse.

'Who?'

'I thought nobody was close. Not within days.'

'There are men within a few days of here?'

'Of course,' he says, so easily. Of course there are others left over, living out their last days. So why do we never see them? I look at Uncle Ted and wonder what else he does in this wood other than gather sticks and hunt rabbits. He meets my gaze and raises his eyebrows.

'Listen,' he says. He switches off the torch and my choice to see is taken away from me. Into my blindness comes the soft, slow, distinct sound of feet in mud. But no, it's too gentle for that, the rhythmic sucking is too liquid. I've never heard it before, and it is getting closer.

'Uncle Ted?'

He does not reply. I remain in blackness. I reach out my arms and take tiny steps forward. Under my feet the mushrooms pop and splatter.

The sucking noise is upon me, loud in my left ear. I turn from it, but it turns with me and softens further to a hum, like a breathing voice, bringing back memories of something like Mother; yes, a mother-sound, humming under her breath, and I cannot run from it. It is my unfamiliar and ancient home and I belong within it.

I sink down to the ground amid the spattered mushrooms and let the mother-hum take me away.

* * *

Pinprick light through a sieve, a scattering of beams inside which the aimless meanderings of motes are illuminated. Beautiful. I watch them. There is no urgency. I feel calm, cosseted. I lie, curled up on my side, my eyes fixed to the ceiling.

Must I move? The feeling of contentment is wearing thin. Yes, I must move. I must get up. I am in a large warm chamber with earthen walls. The dirt bears the marks of rough digging, as if with claws. High above there is the light, coming through what appears to be holes in a woven grass mat. There is no door, but there is a ragged hole in the floor. I move to it, unsure if this is a dream, and find it plunges straight down into an absolute darkness that makes me shudder, recoil.

I am under the earth. Is this my burial? How then can I be calm? I fold back into myself and close my eyes. The ground is yielding. I wish it would swallow me and be done.

\* \* \*

The smell of food cuts through me. Now, somehow, there is food. Three apples and a honeycomb are on the floor next to me. They are a gift, a song of autumn, and I cram the comb into my mouth.

As I eat, the humming returns, pleasant and disjointed. It has no rhythm or tune I can place. Did my mother sing it to me once? Is she coming for me? I want to call out her name. The air is dead here. There is no wind. I can't think.

I eat and listen to the humming, and when the last mouthful of apple is gone, the core and pips inside me, I think of how to tell this story when I get free. Every word I use, every turn of phrase I fit together in my head, is wrong. Am I captured? Can I describe myself as a prisoner? Is this solitary confinement? I have read these terms in the books Miriam kept in the school library, but none of them fit. I feel no desire to go, that's what's missing. This is not against my will. I have no will, except to listen to the hum.

The ground shudders and from the hole climbs a thing. A woman. A thing. It is yellow and spongy and limbed, with a smooth round ball for a head. It is without eyes, without ears. I press myself against the rough wall as it emerges and stands like a human, like a woman. It has breasts, globes of yellow, and rounded hips that speak to me of woman, of want, and that disgusts me beyond words.

I am sick on myself. I soil myself. Everything is beyond my control. My terror is sharp and pungent. The thing stops moving towards me.

I can't take my eyes from it. It is alive; I feel it, alive like a person. Not an animal. It watches me. Without eyes it stares, the smooth yellow flesh stretched over its head.

I try to speak to it but no words come out of my mouth.

A minute passes. Two. Ten. It does not move.

The terror recedes, enough for me to feel the discomfort of my wet shit-and-puke covered clothes. I smell terrible. Everything hurts. My head is banging and my heart won't stop thumping in my chest.

It stays static. I focus on the fingers of the creature. The fingernails are long, curved like talons on a hunting bird. They look delicate, decorative. They are not hands hardened by work. To look at them makes me feel jealous, desirous and protective, all at the same time. Such little hands. If I look only at the hands I feel warmth spreading through me. They are feminine. I haven't seen anything that fits that word for such a long time. These are feminine hands. I feel the urge to touch them.

Revulsion at my own thoughts overcomes me—I am shivering, both cold and hot, and the pain in my head is growing, growing. The thing moves backwards, taking small steps, then drops into the hole and is gone.

Left to my own stench, I curl up and fall, once more, into sleep.

\* \* \*

There follow days and nights with the thing. It comes without warning. Sometimes I awake and find it close. At other times it raises its head from the hole and moves no further. It stays so very still. I think that it is waiting for something. I think it wants me to name it.

It provides me with water and food. It took away my stained clothes and cleaned up after me. I find I can control myself and my thoughts around it if I concentrate on some small part of it. Terror, hatred, panic and those stranger, softer feelings: they are there, but they do not crowd me or make me their puppet. If I want to touch it, I would be able to do so with a clear mind. I think I would like to touch it.

It is sunset. The sieved light has taken on a dusky, pinkish cast and I can picture the others waiting at the fireside, ears attuned to the pops and crackles of the flames, hoping for a story that will not come. Or is someone else telling them tales of the dead? I try to picture Thomas conjuring the peachy skin and red lips of women for their listening enjoyment, and it makes me smile. He would do a grander job of describing an onion and goat's cheese tart.

The ground shudders and the thing emerges. It comes to me, walking with a sway of its soft yellow hips, and stops within touching distance. I repress everything I feel, the horror and the longing. I reach out.

Its own hand stretches out and meets me halfway. Palm to palm.

Cool, almost damp. Smooth and spongy. It is a shock to feel its lack of warmth, but it is not unpleasant. Just different.

The smoothness changes. I feel a raised surface, like gooseflesh, and then the bumps become larger, prickly. The thing hums, high, in pulses; the sound comes from inside it. I'm certain that it's very, very excited. We are excited.

I pull my hand back. The sense of urgency, of delight, that emanated from it vanishes. To touch it—this plant's thoughts, emotions, in my mind. I can't separate its desires from my own.

It keeps its hand still and makes no other move, so I return my hand to it and let it speak to me of longing, of satisfaction, of a long long wait in the dark. At first everything is a rush, but I begin to discern more particular, delicate thoughts, like butterflies dipping to flowers. They brush my mind and I feel hope, that most ethereal of entities. The thing has hope. Or maybe it is my hope, amplified and appreciated; hopes for a world where we have a place, a meaning, a future. Where we all fit. Tessellate.

The wrongness sweeps over me, obliterates the butterflies, leaves only black insect legs, squirming and scrabbling in my mind. This time I push away for good, retreat, wrap my arms around my body and shake my head at it, no, no, until it moves back and leaves me alone.

It drops into the hole, and is gone.

Did my mother hum to me when I was little? Did she touch me, hold me, fill me with her noise and her thoughts? This loneliness I feel is of the womb, borne by women. I was sixteen when they all died and I thought I understood this loss, but it comes to me that I didn't know what women gave to the world. It wasn't about their lips, their eyes or the gentle quality of their voices. It was about the way that all men are a part of them. And now we are part of nothing.

There are no more stories. I can make no words. There are only sounds from deep within my chest, from a cavity that has been lurking inside me, unnoticed, for years. It is a pain so deep, so black, and I cannot bear it. I must fill it, find a way to stop it up. It will devour me.

The thing returns. I watch it crawl up to me, as it takes hold of me in its cold yellow arms and rocks me, all the while humming. Its joy at the knowledge that we are together overwhelms everything, and keeps me quiet.

\* \* \*

My mother was not a beautiful woman in her own eyes. Once, when I was a young boy, I found a magazine under her sleeping bag. It was slippery, glossy, smooth to the touch. Inside were collections of thoughts on how to be thinner, better, happier, as if these things were part of a pattern, like honeycomb. And the women were strange, elongated creatures with diamond faces, their bodies held at odd, difficult angles. I found them disturbing and I asked my mother that night—before I realised that not all thoughts were suitable for mothers—why they made me feel that way.

She told me it was a sign that I was beginning to grow up. 'All men want to look at beautiful women. Especially your father,' she said, with such envy and sadness and disgust in her voice. I could see she wanted to be like those women, although I couldn't understand why. And so beauty became something unobtainable, something to be admired and feared, beyond my reach, even my understanding.

Now, in the thing's embrace, I spend longer there every day, never wanting to be apart from it. I find a name for it. I call it Bee. Bee for Beauty. It is not inaccessible or frightening. Everything it thinks, feels, wants and needs is open to my discernment. Beauty is a word that has a different meaning for me now and I am delighted to have reclaimed it.

Bee is so cool, so soft, like a sponge wrapping itself around me in the midst of a terrible fever. It moulds itself to me, sits

23

astride my lap and takes my cock inside it. I sink into it like pressing into mud and Bee gives, gives, gives until I am fully inside. I feel our pleasure, our amazement, our amplified, doubled joy. We are drawn into ourselves, completely without the world.

Afterwards, when I feel sick at what I have done, Bee hums and soothes me, assures me that it is not unnatural or wrong. It implants strange images in me of earthy darkness, of waiting, growing, moving to sunlight, opening, learning and expanding. Like being a baby in a womb, deep in the mother and unaware of anything but that sharp, tingling and delicious edge of potential.

I know Bee is not alone. It shows me images of others growing from the bodies of women, mingling with their cells, learning about us and themselves. Bee shows me many of them close by, connected in thought, hoping for men to learn to love them and take them into their own.

In my mind I gently show Bee my own initial repulsion once more. Can that be overcome? And yet, why shouldn't it be? If I can overcome this repulsion, so can the others. And my optimism spreads into Bee, infects it too. It stands, lifts me up, and holds me in its arms. Bee is so strong. It drops into the hole and carries me through the darkness, out of a sloping tunnel to where there is sharp sunlight. The frost is sweet like the crunch of apples. And everywhere there are Beauties, yellow Beauties like my love, soft and cold, wanting nothing but to be warmed by men.

\* \* \*

Music. I have missed it. There is more than one way to make a long tale in mind and memory; Landers is playing the guitar and singing while Keith D fiddles. They sing of soul cakes, a winter song, and I realise I have been under the ground for too long. My famous sense of time and place has left me; this is the wrong song for late autumn but it is a good song, one of my favourites. The humanity in me jumps up and begs to draw closer.

But I keep my distance, just out of the light of the flames, and let my eyes play over the familiar faces: William, Eamon, the lads, even Uncle Ted, who looks unchanged except for the sadness that sits on his shoulders.

Why is he here, by the fire? To mourn me? Is that why they play my favourite song and yet nobody dances? I am dead to them. If I do not act now somebody will get up at the end of the song and tell stories of me; *I remember when* and *Wasn't he* and *I'll miss his* and other things that a living person should never hear about themselves in case it changes the way they choose to carry on living.

So I come into the circle.

The music stops. Fingers and mouths are frozen. Even William is without comment. His face is a picture of surprise. Uncle Ted is the first to move. He gets up, takes long strides until he is putting his arms around me so I am pressed to his leather coat.

He is saying, 'Where have you been? Where have you been?' over and over with no pause, no drawing of breath. It brings the Group to life. They rush to me and surround me, talking to themselves, to each other, *Who would have believed, We thought he was, How can he be.* I let their words be a blanket for me, wrapping me in their joy and concern.

Then William is there, pushing his way through to stand toe to toe with me. Uncle Ted lets me go. The others step back.

'Ted said you disappeared. We searched. No signs, no trail. Nothing. Ben and Thomas are gone too.'

'I was kept safe,' I tell him.

William assesses me with his straight gaze, the one he keeps only for important judgements. 'You were kept?'

'Unharmed. All is well. All is good.'

'There are... people in the wood? Another Group? Will they have Ben and Thomas?'

'Not a Group.'

Uncle Ted says, 'Let him get warm, for Heaven's sake,' and pushes William out of the way. He leads me forward to the glow of the fire which is bright against my face. It is an unpleasant sensation after so long in the dampness of the earth; I feel my skin tightening, the hairs on my body lying flat and sleek in response and my pupils contracting.

'I have a story,' I say. 'The story of what happened to me out there.'

'Time for that later,' says Uncle Ted, but the younger ones are already buzzing, settling themselves down, and I know they have missed this. Nobody could take my place. I am given the confidence to tell the story I have been shaping, and they will listen to the end. They will understand what I have to tell them.

\* \* \*

*In the beginning there was a lonely orphan boy. His father was only known to him as a figment of his own imagination and his mother went the way of all women. He mourned them, but not excessively so for he was only as lonely as every other man he knew and it would have been selfish to weep when others must work.*

*So he worked too. He was lucky, he had a talent for tales: long tales, short tales, tales of reality, of mystery and of imagination. The other men recognised his talent and encouraged it. All men should be so lucky, but the truth is—talent does not touch us all. The orphan appreciated this and did not squander his talent or waste his words. He worked very hard to entertain and delight his listeners around the fireside, and his talent and his tales grew a little more every day.*

*It grew, but his talent did not bloom.*

*This bothered him. All organic things grow and reach fruition. He saw this in the earth and the seasons, in the wild flowers and the tame vegetable patch. But what kind of flower would his talent produce? Where do stories lead? The answers he imagined scared him. But his mother had always said to him,* 'Your imagination can take you to the best and worst places. It is a ship on a sea of dreams and it's up to you to steer it.' *And so he tried to control the rudderless boat of his brain, and sweated daily with the effort.*

*It seemed storytelling was as hard a form of work as tilling the soil, in some ways.*

*Years passed. The orphan began to lose the sound of his mother's voice and the movement of her mouth, the colour of her eyes, the feel of her hair. So he held tight to an old photograph, staring at it, carrying it with him, until he realised that the mother he knew had become only the photograph, an image of what a mother should be, and there were no real memories left. On the day of that realisation he took the photograph to the edge of the valley, the steepest cliff that overlooked the sea. He tore his mother's face to pieces and then threw the pieces over the rocks to be carried away, to be truly forgotten.*

*And on that day there came the Beauty.*

*They were found in the graveyard, springing from the decaying bodies of the women deep in the ground, and they were found in the woods, spreading themselves like a rug over the wet earth. The Beauty were small at first but they grew, and they took all the best qualities of the dead. They sucked up through the soil all the softness, serenity, hope and happiness of womankind. They made themselves into a new form, a new birth, shaped from the clay of the world and designed only to bring pleasure to man.*

*But the Beauty knew, from the many experiences of the women that had gone before, that men did not always love what was good for them. Men could attack, hurt, maim and murder the things that came too fast, too suddenly, like love, like beginnings that involved the death of the old way. So the Beauty decided to find a man who could accept them, who could speak for them. And serendipity sent to them the lonely orphan boy.*

*They came across him, lost and wandering in the forest, like a gift, and took him into the earth with them. The Beauty treated him kindly, gave him time to come to appreciate the devotion they offered. They chose one of their number, a patient and wise one with large breasts and a beguiling scent, and sent it to the boy. He recognised the smell and form of woman. His memories were returned to him in that aroma, in the pendulous feel of the breasts, and it was as if his mother had returned to him, as if all of womankind had returned.*

*He did what came naturally to him with this beautiful creature, and soon the shame and guilt he felt at fondling and fucking passed away into death and something else was born in its place: a new delight, unfettered, in such beauty. And, for the first time, hope.*

*So the boy agreed to speak to the other men, to tell them of such happiness and to offer it to them. And they said—*

*They said—*
I stop speaking.

A time passes. The men look at each other. I know they are waiting for me to finish the story, to give it a meaning, but this time around it is not my job to say the final words.

'You aren't finished,' says William.

'No,' I tell him. 'Neither are you.'

And then I see the shapes move from the darkness, coming into the light. William jumps to his feet, then Uncle Ted and the others: all shouting, moaning, pissing and frothing, fighting, struggling, running. The Beauty encircle them, enclose them, take them into their embrace and rock them, absorb them, until terror and pleasure become one and the same. Then the only sounds are the sighs and sobs of wordless confusion that will, no doubt, soon be replaced with an acceptance as deep and wide and thankful as my own.

# PART
# TWO

'The men are unhappy,' says Doctor Ben.

I shake my head. I say, 'No, they're not. They're not able to admit they're happy. That's all.'

Thomas keeps a clean kitchen. The fridge and the oven are old, rust-speckled white-slabbed boxes, side by side like grizzled guard dogs, standing to attention on the tiled floor. The house is old too—a small brick building at the entrance of the Valley, where once a warden lived to watch over nature and protect it from humanity. Or so the story goes.

As the cook, Thomas lives in a kind of luxury here. It is warmer at night than in the huts, no doubt. The otherness of this kitchen, powered by windmills and overlooking the tidy walled garden, is the perfect setting for difficult conversations. The kind that should not be overheard.

'Landers tried to kill himself,' says Doctor Ben.

Thomas stops chopping green beans and turns to us, knife in hand. 'Really?' he says, saucer-eyed.

'He did a bad job of it. One small cut of the wrist. I bandaged it.'

I lean back against the shelves and feel the first twinge of discomfort. Separating from Bee quickly leads to an ache in my stomach, a queasiness that grows with passing minutes. Bee stands on the other side of the kitchen door waiting, along with the Beauties that belong to Doctor Ben and Thomas. As the first three to find pairings, kept under the earth with them, the feeling is strong that we shouldn't be in different rooms, not for a moment. It is this that makes me uncomfortable, but I can appreciate it. Discomfort is not a disaster.

'Landers' Beauty picked him up and carried him to me,' says Ben. 'It refused to let him suffer.'

I say, 'Then it did a good thing, right? It cares for him. They care for all of us.' They have taken over the heavy tasks, the unpleasant ones. They farm and they chop without complaint. And now they save our lives.

'It's my opinion,' says Ben, raising his eyebrows, 'that some of the men will never get over the feeling of revulsion. We can't live like this.'

'Give it time. We got over it, didn't we?'

'You came round in weeks. So did Thomas. It's easier on the younger ones. But we're well into spring now and the older ones are so ashamed still. They don't want it, but they can't refuse it.'

'Is that how you feel?' I ask him. I've seen him struggle to accept the couplings round the fire after my nightly stories, and the way the Beauty simply touch, mould, demand the comfort of our bodies at any time, blocking out all other thoughts. 'Do you wish you'd never met your own Beauty? That you'd never met Bella?'

'Every day,' he says, and I believe him. Ben adds, 'I wish I'd never gone into the wood that night with Thomas to look at the mushrooms. And yet it's not that life was better before. It's that—I can't explain it.'

'Let me explain it for you, around the fire. I can give it a voice.'

'No,' he says. 'No.'

I say, 'Why not? That's my job. I should make a story about

this. It will help us all to face it, overcome it.'

'That's just it, Nathan. Your stories, all of them—they aren't the truth any more. Last night you told the story of the Group, and you made it into... a saga.'

'It is a saga!'

'No! It hasn't all been a journey towards meeting the Beauty. It hasn't been a straight road leading to a dawn. We didn't come to the Valley of the Rocks in order to meet and meld with these—walking mushrooms!'

Thomas snorts.

'It's not funny!' I tell him, but it only makes him worse. He laughs out loud, and in between gasps for air he says, 'Mush... rooms...'

Doctor Ben and I wait for his laughter to subside. When Thomas finally manages to control himself we hear scraping on the kitchen door; our Beauties want in. The urge to go to them is strong, palpable in the room, but none of us move.

Thomas puts down the knife and stares at his fresh spring beans. He has lost weight since joining with Betty. There is a sleekness to his cheekbones, the muscles starting to show through on his shoulders.

'I'm making goat stew,' he says. 'Cooked for hours with green tomatoes from the hothouse, new potatoes fresh from the buckets by the back door and the first green beans plucked from the canes. Topped with griddle bread and melted goat's cheese. One of my favourites. Before all this I would have put in mushrooms. The earthiness gives it something, deepens the taste of the thyme.'

Thomas rubs his thumb and forefinger together. 'Delicious. But I can't. I can't pick a mushroom. It would be like cannibalism. How crazy is that? Cannibalism.' He laughs once more: softly, weakly.

Doctor Ben moves to him and pats him on the shoulder. 'Can you represent this truth in your tales?' he asks me.

I say, 'I can make a story about a boy who went off mushrooms.'

He says, 'That's not what this is.'

'Yes,' I say. 'Yes, it is.'

'Then you see, you misrepresent our history. It's not safe in your hands.'

His words sting me, like bees in my ear. The scratching on the door intensifies. I have to raise my voice to be heard over it.

'I don't hold our past in my hands and I'm not responsible for it. I'm a storyteller. I speak of the deeper truth of our morality; our history should reflect that.'

'No,' he says. 'You represent your own morality, and expect us all to agree with it.'

'Please don't fight,' says Thomas. He is crying. He goes to the door, throws it open and lets in the Beauty. Betty is first. It backs him up against the counter and takes Thomas into itself, wrapping its arms around him. He slumps into its embrace. His trousers work their way down his legs and he thrusts and shudders. Then my Bee is upon me and I don't think about Thomas or Ben any more.

* * *

*To start—*

*There will be love. The word was dead. Then it rose from under the earth, took form, came to us and demanded our attention anew, even though we were not willing to give it. For it is easier to be loveless, to dismiss that tender stretching. The heart is a muscle; when we love, we exercise—we must breathe hard, we must feel the burning of our legs and lungs, we must grow dizzy with it. We must run with this new love until we feel an exhaustion of our souls.*

*There will be change. The word can move from myth to material. We shall weave cloth from it, add squares to the patchwork blanket of our Group. Older squares are fraying and torn; this fresh, clean cloth will comfort us, even if our fingers are pricked in the act of stitching.*

*There will be beauty. The word can be reclaimed from the wasteland of women, from thoughts of the crawling disease that infested wombs. Beauty is here, fresh and willing to hold our hands once more, like a child in a garden.*

*So let us hold hands. Let us join in these final days of our fate. Let us walk together in love, in change, in beauty, on and on until the end.*

\* \* \*

It is early morning and I am looking upon Belinda, lying on the floor of the hut it shared with Hal. Its head is stamped open, its arms and legs ripped off. The stumps drizzle black. The body has been opened with something sharp like a knife, and inside there are grey strings and shapes with the rich smell of the compost heap.

*This death is your fault, Nathan,* the older men will say. *It's on your conscience.*

It's not that I don't have reservations. Perhaps they all think that I am impregnable to their misgivings, but I see it, I see it! We must give up so much of ourselves to the Beauty, and not just our semen. We surrender our independence that was ever the strength of our Group; we make ourselves reliant on their soft sponginess, those blank faces. I feel the same repulsion to this but the truth is—what are we keeping our independence for?

Once upon a time we idolised the past because that was all we had. Now we must look to the future and sacrifice the sacred cow of our glorious Group. We are being made anew. We change, or we die. Or, it seems, we kill.

Once such thoughts have come to me I can't forget them and I know they will work themselves into my stories whether I like it or not. So, instead of waiting for it to trickle out of me, I decided to spurt out my ideas in a new kind of story. A story of the future.

After I finished my new story I was met with a profound silence. My stories normally provoke feelings of friendliness or appreciation. The good will, the gratitude of the Group, has been my reward. But this story did not provoke such feelings. I couldn't say what they thought. But I was sure that they did listen; I felt the disturbance my words caused like the ripples on the surface of a pond after the falling of a stone.

Is this death my fault? Is it on my conscience?

Hal sits in the corner of the hut, eyes closed, face calm, hands clenching and opening. Gareth stands by him, holding a scythe. Of course—not a knife. A scythe. The black liquid coats its edge.

'Why?' says William.

Gareth jerks his head to Hal. 'He asked me to.'

There is a scratching at the door.

'Don't let them in,' says Hal. His hands work against the material of his trousers, picking, picking, picking.

'What can we do?' William asks Uncle Ted. They exchange long looks.

'We have to let them see,' I say. 'What other option is there?'

'Hide it,' says Gareth.

The men, apart from Hal, look around the room as if there is a rug under which this crime could be swept. Hal looks only at me. I think he knows what I am about to do, and his eyes contain a pleading.

I walk over to the door and open it.

Our Beauties do not enter. They sway on the threshold and I wonder—how can they tell? With no eyes, how can they know so quickly that one of their number lies mutilated on the floor?

They make no sound, and neither do we.

I see my Bee, feel my need for it rise up in me. When it does not come to me, I remember the old coldness of my life, and I know I do not want that again, not ever. How could Hal bear to watch his only comfort be destroyed? How could he give that command? There is something at work here that I do not understand and for the first time I am scared. Not of the Beauty, but of my own kind.

Gareth leans the scythe against the wall, then clears his throat. Perhaps he's considering an apology, and I wonder how that would be phrased, but before he can speak the Beauty move backwards as one and walk, at speed, away from us. I step out into the bright sunlight and follow them as they cross the camp, past the huts, past the campfire, their numbers growing, pulling together until every Beauty has collected together and they are retreating past the boundaries of the forest faster than I can run. Then they are gone from sight.

Men come and stand by me on the edge of the tree line. I look amidst the branches but there is nothing, no yellow, no movement. There are only still, brown branches, bearing the buds of spring.

I realise it's only the teenagers who stand with me. Adam, Paul, Oliver and Jason, the ones who used to tease poor Thomas before he became the cook. They always looked like a pack of dogs in my mind, standing together, sleeping in a heap. Now they look like four puppies who have been left behind by their mothers.

'Where are they going?' says Paul. He is dark blond with a long, curved nose and front teeth that protrude in an attractive way, like a spaniel.

'I don't know,' I say.

'What?' says Oliver, the biggest of the Group, the sheepdog with long tangled hair forever in his eyes. 'What?' he repeats.

I say again, 'I don't know.'

There must be other words than this, but I can't find them. There is a hole of dread into which my voice has fallen; I can feel my insides being clawed, raked by the nails of my terror.

'When are they coming back?' says Adam, and Jason echoes, 'When?' They are yapping puppies, black and tan, who may grow fierce one day.

I don't have any words for this.

Other men come to us. I can't explain it; the instinct is strong not to go into the woods. We gather on the edge. Someone calls, 'Hello?' and the sound is swallowed by the trees.

'It was Hal and Gareth,' says a voice behind me that I place as Keith D, the fiddler. 'They killed one of them. Splattered it to bits. Now the Beauty won't come back.'

In the aftershock of these words a feeling is forming—a muttering, a tumult such as I have not felt before. 'They should be punished,' says Paul, with a sword of a voice, and others agree. The Group surges back from the woods, towards the hut. I go with them, trailing behind. I know what's going to happen and although I would like to persuade them from this path, I am dumb.

'It needs a law!' William is shouting. He stands in the doorway of Hal's hut, blocking the crowd's view of the remains of Belinda. 'It needs due process! We cannot simply decide they're guilty. Guilty of what?'

'Murder!' shout the teenagers.

'It's not murder to slice up a plant,' says William, but his face betrays him and the crowd sees it.

Then, from behind him, come Hal and Gareth. They push him to one side and stand, chins up. 'We deserve to be punished,' says Hal. 'We did it. I had to be free. My mother wouldn't have liked it.'

'Do what you like,' says Gareth, only his clenching fists giving away his feelings. 'I'm only sorry I didn't do my own as well. But I couldn't. I'd do all the rest, but not my Barbara.'

'It's murder!' calls Adam, and Jason repeats, 'Murder!' The crowd is building up to something that I do not want to see. It would forever infect my stories.

The bell rings.

It is deep and strong. Uncle Ted stands beside it, on the porch of William's house. The crowd turn to him, fall into silence for him. He looks like a leader.

'A beating,' he says. 'That's the punishment. Ten strokes each with this.' He holds up the stick that usually sits in his belt. 'I'll do it. Then none of you are to blame and it's all done with. I'll do it by the fireside, in plain sight, where the Beauty can see it.'

He walks to the fire, and stands beside it.

The crowd move towards him, bringing Hal and Gareth with them. I go back to the hut instead, where Doctor Ben is still kneeling over Belinda.

He glances up at me. 'Look,' he says.

Outside there is a sound, a meaty thud, followed by another, then another. I put my hands over my ears and turn my eyes to where Doctor Ben points. The mess of Belinda's head is grey, turning black. There is a glimpse of white. Ben moves the grey strands with his forefinger and more white is revealed. It is a jagged piece of bone, curving away. The remains of a skull.

I take my hands from my ears. The punishment is over. The crowd is making strange noises, like the call of birds at daybreak. I go to the door and see the Beauty returning, with my Bee, lovely Bee, coming for me. My body gets hard for her, even as tears start to form in my eyes.

All the delicate thoughts are gone. My whimsies, my long lithe strands of seasons and stories. Gone.

\* \* \*

Uncle Ted seeks me out as night falls. He finds me in the graveyard. His Bonnie and my Bee stand next to each other, humming, while we look at what remains of the graves. The ground is freshly turned over, teeming with worms. If I wasn't here the night-time animals would be feasting.

'Are you glad they're back?' I ask him.

He doesn't reply.

I ask, 'How are Hal and Gareth?'

'They'll heal. I was soft on them. Made it look good for the crowd.'

'You think the younger ones would have…'

He says, 'Don't you?' Ted shrugs, stamps around the grave of my mother. The sky is clear and it will be a cold night. The pinkish cast of the clouds makes everything soft, hazy, like another world.

'No,' I say softly. 'No, I don't.'

'Maybe I know men better than you do then, for all your stories. I know what they're capable of.'

'How do you know?' And then I understand; I can finally put into words what's been bothering me since that night in the woods. I say, 'You knew the mushrooms grew only on the graves of women because you buried women there. In the woods, when I was taken. You led me to the place where you had put women in the ground.'

'Yes,' he says.

'Why didn't you bring their bodies to the graveyard instead?'

'The idea was to keep them out of this place, Nate. Don't you get it? I didn't find them dead. I found them alive. And I killed them.'

'You—' It makes no sense to me. 'But why would you…'

'Three of them. They were heading straight for us. We'd just buried Teresa the week before, the last of our own women. I couldn't risk more of them turning up, making us all feel for them, just to lose them. Just to die.'

I say, 'Maybe they weren't sick!'

He gives me a pitying smile. 'All women were sick. Think about it. Why were they wandering through the woods alone if they hadn't been thrown out of their own town? They'd been sent out there to die by their men.'

'You don't know that,' I whisper. Do I want to hear more? No. Yes. 'How did you…?' My eyes fall to the stick on his belt and he rests his hand on the knobbed end.

'No, I did it kindly. Took them out one at a time, said they needed to be blindfolded to come to us, that we had a cure and needed to be careful about who knew our location. Then I strangled them, quick. They died with hope, which was a gift, wasn't it? I told them a good story, made up on the moment. Worthy even of you.'

'Uncle,' I say. I hold up my hands. 'No more.'

He kicks at the worms with his boot. 'Some of us are born to be free on the wings of imagination and some of us are held down by the chains of reality, isn't that right? No doubt you'd find a better way of saying that. I do the groundwork so you can have your head in the clouds. I don't want praise for it. I do it gladly, for you, for the memory of your mother. I told her I'd keep you safe. Keep you happy.'

'I can't be happy. Not now. Not after today.'

'Melodrama,' he tells me, not unkindly. He adjusts his belt. 'You're proving my point. This will mean something to you and that's fine. Weave the deaths and the beatings into your tales and grow from it. However you want to use it. It means nothing to me.'

'Those women meant nothing to you?' I ask him. I picture his hands on their soft necks, their eyes covered, their heads thrown back.

'Nothing that I'm going to tell you,' he says, and stomps away. Outside the gate his Bonnie waits for him, follows along behind him, not touching him. That is how he likes it, at least in view of the others. Untouchable Uncle Ted.

\* \* \*

I am with Bee, in Bee; it is my only solace, my comfort, my distraction. What did I do before it? How can we need something so badly without knowing that the need exists?

Time has swept clean the cobwebs of panic that trailed across our faces when the women started falling sick. We thought we would all get sick. Men too. Why wouldn't we? We lived in equality, didn't we? It never occurred to us that the disease would not consider us all equal. There were days of hysteria. Hysteria, the sickness of the womb. And yet somehow William kept us together, even as only the women died.

He told us, if there is help, we will find it, and he sent down to the town, to the men in suits who came in their cars and struggled up the rocks to us with sombre faces that gave out the message so clearly that it was no shock that night when William repeated it to us.

'Women everywhere are afflicted. So far there's no cure.'

'Only women?' asked Miriam. I got the feeling she and William had already discussed the matter; the question had been planted to focus the Group's attention on the problem.

'Only women,' said William. Someone moaned, long and deep. A terrible sound.

How I hate the sounds of pain.

Bee hums, and I am soothed. Bee never makes sounds that wound me. Even if I beat out its brains with a rock it would not scream or cry out. None of the Beauty would. They would simply leave, and that is why they are stronger than us. Because they do not have to fight at all. It is my job to make the men understand this. We are weaker than them.

After William's announcement that night, after the Group had wept and railed and attempted to accept the end of half the world, the fireside became a terrible place. Landers and Keith D refused to play, and nobody would have sung anyway. Silence. It is worse than pain. It is my mortal enemy. It kills me, cuts me up, that dread silence of despair. Even back then I couldn't bear it. I was sixteen years old and already an enemy of silence.

And so I stood up and started to talk. Nothing important. Nothing real. What surprised me, as I retold the plot of the book I had just finished reading, in which a boy wizard defeated a great evil, was that nobody stopped me. I talked for hours, and people listened because they hated the silence too. They were happy to create it, and then terrified by what they made. And so I came to understand the split at the root of the soul of all men.

When I ran out of voice, William said, 'That sounds exciting, Nate. Tell us more tomorrow.'

And so I did.

For the first time, tonight, in Bee's arms, I worry that I am running out of stories. What will come out of my mouth? What can I say, in the face of what I have learned today?

Why does it even matter any more? Why, in the face of such suffering, do stories matter?

That is the worst thought of all, the thought I want to claw out of my head, wrap in a sack and throw into the sea.

Bee hums louder in my ear. My skin is pressed so close against its clammy yellow breasts that we are almost one.

'Mother,' I say. 'Mother.'

\* \* \*

'It disgusts me,' says William. 'It should disgust us all.'

Nobody replies. Uncle Ted faces away from us and Eamon and Doctor Ben sit on the floor of the rough wooden lookout platform. I enjoy the view from the treehouse. The weather is warming up. The nettles are young and sweet for soup, and the birds only think of the need to nest. We have all settled into a pattern; we tessellate. It's all I ever wanted, and yet it's not everything. The pattern stretches only so far. I tell my stories every night with increasing desperation.

I preferred speaking about the past. There is so much to say about a past. It is a vein of gold through a mountain, leading to an incontrovertible stone heart of truth. But the future is a horizon—a faintly visible line that may promise much, and always remains too far away to touch. My eyes hurt from trying to see it clearly. And so much depends on me now.

I found some dark glasses of my mother's amongst her old clothes and have taken to wearing them, much to William's disapproval. The teenagers have gone one step further. They wear skirts, and cite the ease of joining with their Beauties—no more zips to undo, simply lift the material!—and the coolness that will benefit their packets as the summer approaches.

If it were only teenagers I don't suppose William would be too offended. But it's also Thomas, who spends all his time in a pink dress with puffed sleeves, a row of white buttons down the front as delicate as daisies. I burst out laughing the first time I saw him in it and he smiled, his cheeks reddening.

'I know,' he said, 'don't laugh. Honestly. Trousers have been cutting into my stomach.'

It was a feeble excuse, given that he has been losing so much weight recently. I raised an eyebrow at him, and he added, 'Betty likes it too.'

'How can you tell?'

'Can't you?' he said, and I had to admit he was right. Betty stood in the corner of the kitchen and hummed with a contentment that sounded like a cat's purr.

Since then, two weeks ago, I haven't seen Thomas out of that dress. Perhaps that's the reason William called this emergency meeting. What I don't understand is why I've been invited.

'It's not right to wear them,' says William, when nobody rushes to agree with him. 'It's disrespectful.'

'There's nobody left to disrespect,' says Eamon. 'Look at us. We're shagging mushrooms. Do you really think respect is an issue any more?'

Below us, at the bottom of the tree, the Beauty wait. As usual. They stand so still. They are expecting me to speak for them.

'They're not mushrooms,' I say.

William raises his head and glares at me. 'Don't even start,' he says.

'Don't I have the right to speak any more?' I ask him.

'We all know where you stand. You've spent enough time trying to persuade us that this is part of some grand plan.'

'I don't want to speak on that matter,' I say. 'This is about something else.'

'We're not here to jump to your—'

'Let him speak,' says Ted, from where he leans against the trunk of the tree.

William opens his mouth and then closes it.

'The Beauty are intelligent,' I say. 'They communicate with each other. They communicate with us too, although we pretend not to hear. They are—they are our women reborn.'

'They are not,' says Eamon. 'That's a lie.'

I say, 'I don't lie.'

'That's all you do!' he says.

'Wait,' says Doctor Ben. 'He's not lying. Not exactly.' He clears his throat and hugs his knees. 'After the incident involving Hal and Gareth, investigation of the... remains suggested that some of the bones of the deceased have been incorporated into the, err, the Beauty. Most notably the skull and the spine. I don't know if they're all the same. Maybe it was a random occurrence with that one.'

'Belinda,' I supply. Its name was Belinda, before its head was smacked into pieces.

Nobody speaks. Eamon stretches out his legs, stands and begins to descend the ladder. At the bottom his Beauty—Bree—comes to him, arms open, and he pushes it away with a great shove so strong that it falls backwards and sprawls on the ground. I didn't know Eamon was so strong. He walks away and Bree picks itself up and follows after him.

'So they've used some old bones,' says William, and his voice shakes. 'That changes nothing.'

'They sprang from women,' I say. 'We use them like women. They are women.'

'They are not, and we will not call them such.'

'They're not women, Nate,' says Uncle Ted. He turns to me and I see a great weariness in his face. 'You had a mother, but not a wife. You don't understand the difference between it. I don't say this to take anything away from you. You must trust those who remember all of womanhood, not just the hugs of a mother.'

Am I missing some element of love? The Beauty offer comfort, sex and softness. What else is there? And how can Uncle Ted say he knows these things and I don't? There are things he has seen, times he has experienced, that I never will—I give him that. But his capacity to hurt, to kill—is that what he thinks makes him a real man? If so, I will never be a real man and I am glad of it.

'Regardless of what they are,' says Doctor Ben, 'we must draw up rules of conduct. The mark of humanity is how it treats the world and those who share it with us—and the Beauty are alive. Whatever they are, they're alive.

'We started this Group to live by a set of principles. We grow our own food. We replace what we use. We protect what we rear. Now we have taken the Beauty into us. The Beauty deserve to be treated with respect for our sake, if not for theirs.'

William turns on him, his yellowed teeth bared. 'You didn't start this Group at all,' he says. And that is when I know he has forgotten how to be a leader.

I look at Uncle Ted, and he returns my gaze. Then he says, 'William, that remark is unworthy of you.'

William does not reply. He shrinks down into himself, getting smaller and smaller, and I know he feels it inside. He is not fit to lead us any more. When Ted says, 'Right then, let's draw up a list of rules and Nate can read it out tonight, exactly as it's written down,' William does not object, and as smoothly as that power changes hands.

I feel the inspiration of it. Glorious revolution. The schoolbooks talked of it, heads chopped off and crowds baying, and yet all the stability of my world only needed a few words to be wiped away. It didn't even need a story.

And I am at this meeting to witness it. Ted wanted me here, not William. He wanted me to see the change in power and to understand that I am now his mouthpiece.

My freedom is gone and we are being led by a killer.

\* \* \*

To start—

There were no rules. Rules were not necessary. There was man, and there was work and there was plenty. Plenty does not mean riches. There was simply enough. Abundance would have created inequality.

But there was loneliness too. Deep in the bones and brain there was loneliness, in a world of seed and egg, of bee and flower, of pairs. To be a man was to find a hole inside and *know it could never be filled.*

*Until the coming of the Beauty.*

*They grew from the soil and understood without needing words or guidance. They took a form pleasing to man's eye and came amongst him, walking into his garden. And there was much fear at first. Man trembled at the new, the unknown. They couldn't recognise the gift they had been given, even though they took it in their arms and pressed it to their hearts. They were no longer alone, and it was a hard thing to understand.*

*But then they began to see. Spring came and the birds nested. The hares boxed and the feelings rose up strong in man again. Feelings of love. They began to look at the Beauty and see wealth. Riches.*

*And then man divided into men. Some men saw their fortune and rejoiced in it. But other men felt their fear grow stronger—fear of what they were being given, what they would have to pay for it and what might be lost. And they looked out at the innocent Beauty and brought violence and pain into their gardens, not through deliberate murderous intent, but through the sickness in their souls.*

*The sickness led to further division. Should they banish the Beauty and be lonely just so violence could not find them? Or should they face their fear and overcome their instincts? It was too big a question to answer.*

*But the men had an ally. They had reason. Reason, the greatest gift ever given to them. They could think and think again, and in the thinking there lay solace from simply feeling. If they were at war with their emotions, thinking was the best weapon they possessed.*

*We are reasonable men. We can think of a path that may, one day, lead to a solution that eases us all.*

*Here is the path:*

*We will not kill the Beauty.*
*We will not hurt the Beauty deliberately.*
*We will not steal another man's Beauty.*
*We will attempt to be honest in all dealings with the Beauty.*
*We will not speak ill of another man because of how he chooses to deal with his Beauty.*
*We will hold true to these tenets, for the good of the Group, for now and forever, and on, and on, until the end.*

\* \* \*

'I told them,' I say to Bee, from deep within its embrace. 'And now Ted wants to see me.' Am I to be punished? The thought of it won't leave me.

It feels like three o'clock in the morning. My mother used to say that whenever you wake in the dead of night it's bound to be three o'clock, it's just the way it is, and the hands of the clock move slower at that time than at any other. We never had a clock so I couldn't say, but it is a three-o'clock feeling for sure. More and more of what my mother used to say is returning to me.

My tent hut is warm, my blankets piled high. Bee's skin is clammy, but I'm used to that. I am comfortable, surrounded by the things I love, the books I have been allowed to take from the school over the years, because nobody else was interested. Some are stolen, I admit; a blind eye was turned by my old teacher Miriam, no doubt. I miss her knack of knowing me and looking like all the answers of life belonged to her, even the impossible ones. I am an adult now and I feel no such surety; I hope I fake confidence as well as she did.

Perhaps that is the role of a responsible person—to fake

the confidence he doesn't feel so that the young can believe in something. Except there are no young ones any more. I'm not sure who I'm faking for.

'Is it for you?' I ask Bee, and it strokes my face, putting visions in my head of a masterwork of flesh and yellow, a tower built of our bodies, extending out of our arms and legs to form fresh joints, bones, limbs and even mouths that hum to make a symphony of such beauty that it hurts to hear it. The tower reaches to the sky where all is clear, and down below, under the soil, there are roots that stretch as deep as the tower is tall. Deeper, even, to the great heart of our beating planet. Between us all we make the base and pinnacle of Man and Beauty.

'How?' I say to Bee.

It shows me clouds speeding by, days and nights, the movement of the earth, years and years, wrapped and folded like a gift.

'Men age,' I whisper. 'Men die.' How can we unite in this way, build to harmony? The Beauty will outlive us, but we have only this generation. There will be no more.

I receive in my mind's eye a picture of Thomas. He cooks in his kitchen kneading bread, his cheeks reddened with the effort, wearing his mother's dress. He looks—I can't describe it. There is an aura that surrounds him. I feel the expectation of the Beauty has settled on him. He will do something of phenomenal importance.

'What?'

But I don't understand the images I am being shown. The speed of them, the blurs of browns and reds and yellows, the streams of these colours running together. The patterns take me down and Bee hums on. I can feel its pleasure as it lulls me, like a baby, to sleep.

\* \* \*

'We're very disappointed in you,' says Uncle Ted.

I don't know who he means with his *we*. He stands alone, his hand resting on the stick in his belt.

I remember a story my mother told me about my uncle, set back in the time when they were children, living in a suburb with a mother and a father of their own, like in the creased pages of the picture books on the back shelf of the classroom. 'A suburb was like a village,' she said, 'but with spidering roads through it that took people in and out of the nearby city, like blood to a heart.'

Cities are pumps, in my head. They beat with vibrant life, but nobody can stop flowing around the complex chambers and ventricles. There must always be movement or there is death. I imagine they must all be as still and brittle as skeletons now—those great cities of the past.

My mother said Uncle Ted ran away to the city. She never told me why; she made it sound like a whim, but I wonder now what kind of pressure could have made him move inwards to that heart. She said he came back three months later, thinner and older. Time had moved in a different way for him in the city. It speeds and slows depending on where you are, and who you are with.

This morning, time has stopped.

Why is Uncle Ted in this house? Usually I would ask the questions that come to me: Are you living here? Where is Thomas going to live? I want to speak of the importance of Thomas, of the need to protect him, cherish him. And I also want to ask—why must my Bee wait outside, on the other side of the door, while his Beauty stands here in this room, behind him?

But I say nothing. Because this room, this table, the way the chairs are set and the look on Ted's face, make it impossible to speak.

I'm wrong. Time has not stopped. It has reversed. My uncle is a man and I am a boy again, and everything about this room makes me feel it.

He says, 'It was made clear to you to speak only of the rules. To make the rules plain for all.'

Uncle Ted flicks his fingers from his stick. Am I meant to speak? Is this time that is allotted to me? All the reasons I had in my head for what I did have vanished. I am a dandelion clock. One breath from Ted and I am scattered.

'Dandelion,' I say.

'What?'

'Thoughts fly if you breathe too hard. The rules are a shout, but the story is a sigh. This way they do not scatter. They keep their shape, and only bend in the breeze.'

'Is that right?' says Ted.

This is not what I wanted to say. I wanted to make it clear that I have very little power over the story. It must come out as it does. I have been unfaithful to my gift by suggesting that it is under my control. If it can be controlled by me, then I can be controlled by others. I know my uncle is too clever to miss this. I can see from the way he cocks his head that he has not.

'You know this business of stories better than me,' he says. 'I never had much use for them. Perhaps you're right. But I'm sure you realise how much relies on you in this difficult time.'

I nod. He places manacles on me, weighing me down with responsibilities he usurped, and all I do is nod. My cowardice shames me, and yet, even as I berate myself, I hear in my head the sound of his stick on flesh and I cringe away from that memory.

'Let me tell you what's happening, Nate,' he says. 'For your own good. A council has been formed. William, Eamon, Ben and I will steer our Group through this, keep violence under control and help make a new way to live. You brought the Beauty among us and I don't blame you. Nobody blames you. But you must understand that there are those among us who want to tread them back down into the mushrooms they sprang from.

'So we must find a way to control ourselves and the Beauty. And when you remake the past and take potshots at the future in your stories, you play with a delicate balance. You could tip us into chaos. Now, I know that isn't your intention, and that is why we've had this talk privately. Next time you tell a story and I don't like the meaning, you'll be up in front of the Council and there will be punishment.'

'So the Council agrees with you about this?' I ask. Council. That's a word that belongs in books of civic duty and from a world we wanted no part in. I can't believe William would sit on a council, let alone use the word. This is a temporary peace at best, no matter what Ted might want.

He says, 'They do.'

I say, 'You are a judge now?' He frowns at me, and the familiar expression frees my tongue. I am no slave of his. 'You need a curly wig. You need a black flapping robe, like a crow. You are more than one man?'

'We have to be more than men now, Nate, and you have only yourself to thank for that responsibility. Did you really think this way would be better? Fucking plants that bear the shape of the dead; this is what you bring us to. And then you ask us to be happy about it. Well, I'll try to make it stick, for the sake of your mother. She was just like you. She didn't understand about consequences. It was always my duty to keep her safe and now I'll keep you safe too, whether you like it or not.'

I walk up to the long table; I feel it under my hands, so smooth, this new mark of power. I wish for the strength to take it up, to break it with a sudden snap as clean as the breaking of bone.

I say, 'She didn't understand because you were always there to do it for her, is that it? Did you bring her here because you saw the cities out there and found them lacking? And now you want to do the same for us all—protect us from what could be terrible and beautiful and all the things in between, the things that live on and live on. But maybe we want to live on with the Beauty. Maybe we don't want your protection.'

Uncle Ted smiles at me. He is not in the least angry.

'Nate,' he says. 'You're not more than a man after all. You're less than one. You always will be. It's not about what people want. It's about what they need to survive. For us all to survive. You're all so weak that you'll pine away if the Beauty leave, so I'll find a way to make this sorry remains of life work. And in return you'll do as you're told and be grateful for it. You'll start by telling a story of the past tonight and you won't meddle with it: Tell the story of how the Group started. And you won't mention this conversation, or the Beauty.'

'I don't—'

He walks around the table and puts an arm around my shoulder, holding tightly, steering me to the door. 'Enough.'

I want to say more. I want to. I want to. But his words are strong. Want has nothing to do with it. If I am to be a man I must give up on want. I must be more.

It comes to me that maybe I don't want to be a man.

On the other side of the door, Bee is waiting with Doctor Ben and his Bella. Ben wears an expression that makes me forget my thoughts.

'How is he?' says Uncle Ted.

'He's up and about,' says Ben. 'In the kitchen, of course. He said he had to make soup for lunch.'

'You're sure it's a tumour?' he asks Ben.

Ben nods.

Time, that slippery fish, has shot past my guard once more and my hands are empty, clutching at meaning. 'Thomas?' I ask.

'It's bad news,' says Doctor Ben. Ted's grip on my shoulder tightens. It is painful. 'A fast-growing cancer of the bowel.'

I say, 'No.'

'He collapsed late last night, after your story. Thomas says there's no pain. But it's eating up his strength. Still, you can't stop him cooking.'

I wrestle free of Uncle Ted's grip; in his eyes I see surprise at my sudden strength. I say, 'You didn't tell me.'

Ted says, 'You've just been told now.'

'He's my friend,' I say. Doesn't Ted even understand the word?

'Go see him,' says Ben. He stands aside and I walk past to Bee, who stands waiting for me without concern. I don't hear it, but I know it's following me down the hall to the kitchen where I find Thomas chopping an onion with a speed that amazes me. The noise of the knife is like a woodpecker, white flakes of onion flying up from the blade.

My Bee goes to his Betty by the sink and they hum together, complacent, a soothing sound. Thomas uses the flat of his knife to scrape the onions into his pot on the heat and they sizzle; the smell hits me, an instant panacea. What can be wrong in the world when onions fry?

Then he turns to me, and I see how his face has shrunk in on itself overnight, the skin pulling back, giving him a beaky nose, a stretched forehead. And he is bending to one side, as if a force pulls at him. Under his apron, on his left hip, there is a bulge and it is as if his entire body is curving to it, favouring it, making him into a question mark.

'Don't worry,' he says. He takes up a wooden spoon from the drawer and turns back to the onions. The Beauty hums on. The room is hot and pleasant, with the wooden surfaces and the gleaming dip of the sink. I have never seen death. I have spent time in the graveyard and felt the desiccated remains of death—the dry, cold taste of it as it travels through your veins in shreds, blocking you up, slowing you down. Death is not lurking in this room. This is life. The yellow glow of the leaves through the window is life.

I understand what Bee showed to me last night.

I leave the kitchen and find Uncle Ted and Doctor Ben in the hall, deep in quiet conversation. They stop talking as I approach. I know I must look strange to them with my happiness shining out of me, as bright and hopeful as sunrise.

'It's not a tumour,' I tell them.

Ben shakes his head. 'Nate, there's no escaping the fact that there's a growth in the bowel that will, in a matter of months—'

I repeat, 'It's not a tumour.' I can't contain the words any longer. They are the best words I've ever spoken. 'It's a baby.'

# PART
# THREE

I lie in a proper bed, blankets piled high against the cold, Bee beside me, and I think of the line.

The line is invisible, but it exists. It runs from the edge of the wood, through the centre of the campfire, to the graveyard. On one side there is William's hut, the communal huts, the school hut and the fields, and on the other side there is the big house where Ted now lives with Thomas. And where I spend all my time, waiting for a miracle.

For the birth of this baby will be the miracle that will unite us once more. The line draws its strength from its invisibility. Nobody wants to talk about it and I am forbidden to mention it, so the line grows longer and stronger. William, Eamon, the farmers, the older men: they all think there will be no baby and they hate the idea that there could be hope. Because hope takes the form of a joining rather than a continuation.

We will meld to grow. Part human, part Beauty. Could anything be more wonderful, more terrifying? The offer of salvation in the form of a baby who is not a baby. I can finally begin to understand why men kill.

And yet Uncle Ted, the killer, stands firmly with us as a protector of Thomas, never leaving him, grim-faced whenever one of the others approaches. I don't understand this change in Ted. But then, his motives have never been up for untangling. For all his calmness, I feel there is a mess of man underneath. He loves, he hates, he hides the emotions where he thinks nobody can see. And then his eyes burn and his lips draw up, like a threatened dog.

It has occurred to me that my mother was afraid of Ted, of what he might do to others if he thought they were drawing too close to something. To what?

It has been a long six months of consideration and revelation for me; and in that time Thomas has swelled, not to the front like the pictures of pregnant women in the books, but to the side, low on his hip, then pushing out his stomach and distorting his chest. He wears the dresses that once belonged to Miriam—she was a large woman—and still he cooks on, with no perturbation on his face. Thomas emits a serenity that affects all who spend moments with him.

It sneaks into my bland stories of the past, stories that have become more and more fantastical. I tell stories of fairies and goblins, and tea parties for trolls, while the real meanings pretend to be invisible. The goblins go to war or the fairies squabble over a golden crown, hidden deep in the woods. And meanwhile the meanings squat low, so low in the words, that Ted cannot complain.

William and Eamon sit on one side of the fire and we sit on the other, and everyone listens to my stories, long serials that go on night after night. They all wear the expression of hearing pleasant diversions.

We have become excellent liars all round.

Sleep is a truth that will not come readily to those who fill their minds with pretence, so I sit up and watch my breath billow out into the December cold. Then I get up, wrap myself in one of my blankets and think of hot milk in the kitchen, the warm froth of it. One of the delights of living in the big house is the ease of raiding supplies.

Bee sits up and I send it an image of milk. It lies back

down with a low hum. In the past months it has become less interested in staying beside me at all times. We can spend a few minutes apart; we no longer even meld every day. That flush of first need has mellowed into a companionship that brings its own pleasures. I could never be without my Bee, but physical presence is not always necessary. I've noticed the same with some of the other Beauties, such as Ted's Bonnie, but by no means all.

As I tiptoe down the stairs it occurs to me that the Beauty are showing differences between themselves. Could it be that this has always been the case and I simply didn't know them well enough to see it? I don't think so. Maybe they are no longer of one mind. Like the Group, there are fresh divisions. We grow and change—all of us. Will we all grow together?

The smooth surfaces of the kitchen still this thinking. I find the milk jug and pour a little into a small pan, then place it on the cooker. The bottom of the pan makes a hiss as it connects with the heat. It must still have been wet from washing. I picture Thomas methodically cleaning up late at night after my story, finding peace in his movements. For a moment I am jealous of him.

The moon is bright and full through the window. I look on it and see a forever face, a permanence. Some things will always remain the same.

In the stillness it comes to me that I am not alone.

I go to the pantry and listen by the door. Is that breathing I hear? I open the door and at first there are only the black lines of the shelves against the grey jumble of the night. And then I see Thomas. He is crouching, his back against the bottom shelf where the large jars of pickled onions live. His hands are over his face, but I know him.

Betty stands beside him. It takes a step forward, radiating

energy, and I get the feeling that it might be about to hit me. 'I won't hurt him,' I tell it, and it stands back and lets me through. I kneel down and put my blanket around him; he is a puddle on the floor in his floral dress, with his big white socks and his blue knitted jumper. I say words of comfort and feel them sink into him, penetrate his misery and bring him back to himself. Eventually he drops his arms and I sit back on my haunches.

'It's freezing in here,' I say.

Thomas says, 'It's a larder. It's meant to keep the food cold.'

'I know that.'

'Help me up.' He holds out his hands, and it takes all my strength to pull him to his feet. Then I collect the blanket from where it has fallen and try to put it around his shoulders once more, but he shrugs it off. 'Too hot anyway,' he mutters. 'You have it.'

But his skin is so cold as I help Thomas to the kitchen. Should I call Doctor Ben? But he has washed his hands of us, that is what he said to Ted. 'I can't treat a patient who doesn't believe he is sick,' Ben said.

Besides, he thinks Thomas is dying. He stays true to his diagnosis.

The milk has bubbled over in the pan. Thomas tuts. 'I'll have to clean that up tomorrow.' He props himself against the sink and I pour the milk into a mug. When I hold it out to him he shakes his head, so I sip it and feel it as a solid, welcome heat in my mouth and between my hands. Another thing I can be sure of.

'I'm an idiot,' Thomas says.

'Nothing new there.'

'Well, now I'm a bigger one than usual.' He pats the soft

roundness of himself with gentle hands. 'A huge one.'

'Does it hurt?' I ask him.

'No. But it makes me… slow. And awkward. And I can't sleep at night for its turning and poking.'

'It moves inside you?'

'All the time, but worse at night. Sometimes I love it and sometimes…' He looks at Betty, who has emerged from the pantry and shut the door behind itself. '…I hate it and I want it out of me. It drains me. I can't explain it.' His face contorts again. 'It makes me so ugly.'

I put down the mug and give him my most serious face. 'I hate to tell you this, Thomas, but you were always ugly.'

He punches my arm. It actually hurts.

I say, 'Ow!'

'You deserve it.'

I move to the window and relish the constant moon. The garden is flat and leafless, like a picture. Nothing moves. I wish I could speak to my moon, charm it, make it smile.

'What's going to happen?' says Thomas.

'With you, or with everyone?' I ask.

'I don't know. Both.'

I understand what he wants from me. I say, 'You'll have this baby and it will be—it will be—people will take one look at it and they will realise that it needs our love, our unity. Babies bring people together. That's what they are for. Everyone celebrates the arrival of a baby. I read that somewhere.'

'And everyone will love it?' Thomas says, a husk, waiting for me to fill him with hope.

'Everyone.'

'But it will be mine.' He puts his hands on the swelling and his face becomes peaceful as he closes his eyes. Is he trying to communicate with it in the way that I communicate with my

Bee? Are pictures passing between them? After a moment he opens his eyes, and says, 'How come you're so sure?'

'Sure of what?'

'That it is.' He makes a gesture, palms unfolding, like the blooming of a flower between his fingers. 'Is a baby.'

'I just am. And so are you.'

'You're my confidence,' he says. 'You're my confidence, Nate.' He reaches for my hand, and squeezes it.

'Get some sleep,' I tell him. 'Let Betty put you to bed.'

Betty comes forward, and scoops him up. He sighs. I think he might sleep now.

I return to my room to see Bee lying there, and my space in the bed beside it. For the first time I ask myself—is that truly where I belong? Is Bee an integral part of me?

I am Thomas's confidence and Bee is mine. But what if Bee has lied to me, just as I have lied to Thomas? I can't bear to think of it, of Thomas's hands on that swelling and Doctor Ben saying there is no hope. And I doubt. I doubt.

Once, in the school allotment, when Paul and Adam mixed up all the labels on the seeds for a joke, Miriam made it their job to care for all the seedlings personally until they could identify them all. It took them months and every time they asked Miriam for help, she said, 'You made that bed, now you have to lie in it.' It became a well-worn phrase for a while, behind her back, although I'm sure she heard us whispering it, trying to emulate her teaching tone.

There are two types of understanding in this world. There's the kind that comes from the reading and the hearing, and it doesn't penetrate the skin. It is surface knowledge, like a soft blanket that can be placed over the shoulders. And then there is the understanding that comes from doing. That kind of understanding is not soft. It is water that soaks into the rocks and earth, and makes the seeds grow. It is messy, and painful, and impossible to hold.

I get back in my bed. I lie in it.

*　*　*

Thomas moans deeply. The sound, dense with pain, fills his small room. It sinks into his peeling wallpaper and the thrown-back bedsheets.

I talk to him, but he is in a place beyond listening. I say ridiculous, hopeful things, as the skin over his left hip suppurates and oozes, a red mess of blood and pus. Doctor Ben examines it. From my position, sitting next to Thomas's head, I have a view of Ben's expression and also down the length of Thomas's naked body. The swelling is giant, grotesque, the wound on it sickening. Nobody knows how it happened. There were screams in the early morning and I found him this way, Betty hovering over him, shaking its featureless head back and forth.

Thomas's shiny skin is pulled tight across his chest and stomach, stretched to the point of splitting. But my eyes are not drawn to this as much as to his cock and balls. The balls are shrivelled like walnuts, tiny, in a wrinkled pouch that nestles under a tiny worm of a cock. There's no hair on him there. And the smell is so sweet and terrible, like death.

Bee, Betty and Bella squeeze up against each other in the corner of the room, blocking the light from the window so we are in semi-darkness. They are motionless. I can see now how it is possible to hate them. Did Betty do this to Thomas, or is this suffering part of the coming of the baby? Is this part of their plan? His eyes roll back in his head and he moans again. I have to say something. I have nothing to say.

'Thank you for coming out,' I say to Doctor Ben.

He nods. I think my desperation persuaded him to attend.

'The injury must have happened days ago. It's become infected,' he says.

'No. He was fine yesterday.'

Ben shakes his head, then says, 'Can you hold him down? You'll need to be strong.'

'I'll try.' I clamp my hands on Thomas's shoulders, try to prepare myself to put my weight against him. Ben lowers one hand on to the swelling. It could only be a light touch, but Thomas lets out a noise that I have only heard animals make, a cry beyond meaning, and the vast lump inside him moves, independent of his body, rippling under Ben's hand.

Ben falls back, stumbles, and I can't hold Thomas. He has a strength that I could not have imagined as he pulls himself up from the bed and throws me off. He turns on to his knees so that he is crouching, and Thomas puts his own hands to his wound and pulls it apart.

I see his fingers reach in, peel back the skin and dig through the thick yellow mess that spills out of him, coming free from his body, hanging in strands and globs and soaking into the sheets. He pulls free a solid, grey-streaked mass and it falls on to the bed. It writhes and flails and Ben cries out, a noise of such terror. He gets to his feet and reaches out to the mass. Thomas screams.

The Beauties move so fast that my eyes see it as a trick in the dim light. Two of them take Ben's legs while the third puts its hands on either side of his head, and squeezes. There is the sound like a cracking of an egg, and then Ben is gone. He is all gone. His eyes and nose and mouth are gone to pieces, a mess, and all I can recognise is the tangle of grey hair that my Bee scoops up in its hands and carries from the room. Bella takes the rest of Ben, carried in its arms. I am left alone with Thomas, Betty and the thing on the bed.

The baby.

Thomas's eyes are clear and free from pain. He sits back and gathers the baby to his chest. And it is a baby, recognisable in its arms and legs, its scrunched-up eyes and moving mouth. It lets out a noise that is undoubtedly a baby noise. I saw a brand-new baby once before, all pink and swaddled, when I was very young, and it was being passed around a room filled with women who softly held it close. I'm certain that's what this is. A baby. A baby. The word is a delight in my mind. The baby's skin is yellow, as yellow as the Beauty, but in every other way it is a baby.

'It's a girl,' says Thomas.

I don't even understand. 'A girl,' I repeat. Yes, between the legs there is a smooth, split bud. A vulva. A vagina. A womb. This baby has a womb.

He breathes out, and Betty comes to him and puts its head on his shoulder, close to the baby. I move back from the bed to give them some time together and I look at Thomas's wound. Yellow mucus has formed a crust over his hip and there is no blood, no visible injury. I think Thomas will survive this.

Instead, as Betty hums to its newborn daughter, I realise I have a new fear growing inside me, ready to end everything that I thought I once knew.

\* \* \*

*...and the man and his wife of clay, who was a present from the earth itself, wanted a baby so badly that the man ripped at his flesh, crying out in need.*

*Then a miracle happened.*

*He took a handful of his flesh and it transformed, before his eyes, into a child that was half of the clay and half of the man. It was a girl, a gift beyond price. The man and his wife loved their baby girl instantly and were overjoyed, but then it came to them that not everyone in their village would rejoice with them. There were those who rocked jealousy in their arms each night, and those that fed hatred in their bosom. Did they harbour enough of these terrible emotions to hurt an innocent baby? Surely nobody could be that scared, that jealous, that evil?*

*So the man called a meeting and held the new baby up high in the firelight, so everyone could see how tiny and beautiful she was.* Look at my baby, *the man said. And everyone was struck afresh by the miracle of new life, and they swore to protect her from that moment on, and on, and on, until the end.*

On cue, Thomas comes forward and I retreat from the centre of the circle so that all eyes are on him, and the bundle he unwraps. In the glow of the fire, that yellow skin is the colour of butter, warmer than the mustard skin of the Beauty. She is getting lighter.

She starts to cry, from the cold no doubt. There is a frost tonight and the circle is tight, so I can see everyone's face clearly as they look at the arms and legs, the head, the littleness of the limbs. The Beauty sit outside the circle, as usual, in their own Group—but all their bodies are turned to the baby.

'This is Holly,' says Thomas, with the pride of a father. 'Merry Christmas to us all.' He covers his baby over. Behind him, Betty hums with pride. I like to think it's pride.

William is disgusted and Eamon is mirroring his

expression. Such ugliness. But Ted sits beside William and his face is thoughtful. He does not speak. Nobody speaks. I feel the knife that separates us keenly. Can Holly heal this wound?

'Are you trying to feed us this shit, Nate, and make us like the taste?' says Gareth. His face does not give away disgust. He and Hal are stuck fast to their hatred of the Beauty. They are dangerous men.

I glance at Ted, but he does not move. 'It's only a story,' I say. 'Just to help us along the way.'

'And what if nobody wants to go your way?'

Thomas falls back to Betty's side and it puts its arms around him and the baby. I feel the tension in the Beauty growing. Bee and the others raise the tone of their humming, just a little.

I say, 'You can do what you like, Gareth, as long as you let others do the same. Live and let live.'

'Like they did with Doctor Ben?' Gareth asks.

The Group is silent. I feel the knife of their attention pressed against my neck. I say, 'That was an accident.' And maybe it was. I would love to be sure that it was— that he had deserved what happened. The Beauty must have seen in his mind and known his intention. Of course, that must be true. It would make it easier to forget kind Doctor Ben, my friend in days gone past, who now visits me in my sleep and watches me with accusatory eyes in a disembodied head.

'Hal and I saw them burying that accident, and his head was ripped clean off. He didn't want that thing you call a baby to live, so they got to him first.'

'He threatened the baby,' I say.

Gareth says, 'He swore an oath to take care of all human

life! If he was prepared to kill it, then he knew it wasn't human.'

I hear approval in the murmurings of the Group. Gareth is gaining ground. If I can feel danger in the air, then so can the Beauty, and I know how far they'll go to protect Holly.

'Listen,' I say.

'We've had enough of your stories!' calls Hal.

'Then let me tell you straight that you'll all die.'

The Group quiets. They want brutality tonight, either in words or actions, so I'll give them what they want. I continue, 'When you killed one of the Beauty, Gareth, they didn't retaliate. And we made laws to deal with such things. Well, now the Beauty have made their own law. Nobody will harm that baby. Nobody will touch that baby without the permission of the Beauty, or they will rip off your heads. It's their future as much as it's ours.'

Ted stands up in the silence. Everyone looks to him. 'It's a new rule,' he says. 'The Council will ratify it.'

'No,' says William. 'No, they won't.'

He leaves the circle. Eamon follows, then Hal, Gareth and others—mainly the elders. Their Beauties do not go with them. They stay, gathered together, close to Thomas and the baby.

Ted sits back down and puts his head in his hands. We, the remains of the Group, watch him. I want him to do something, say something. I want him to be stronger than ever before, but he does not speak.

In the end it's Thomas who breaks the spell.

'Holly's getting cold,' he says. 'I need to take her inside.'

'Did it hurt?' says Adam, suddenly. He and the teenagers have all stayed.

'I've never felt pain like it,' says Thomas. 'It was like dying.'

'As bad as that?'

'But it healed so quickly. And then it was like it never happened. I know it was terrible, but I can't remember what the pain was like. It's strange.'

Adam and Paul exchange long looks. 'And do you love the baby?' says Paul.

Thomas says, 'Oh yes. She makes my life complete.'

At least I got something right tonight.

Adam and Paul whisper for a moment. Then they stand up together, and throw off the blankets they have been wearing over their shoulders. They both wear thick woollen dresses, and the bulges on their left hips are small, but visible.

'Oh Jesus,' says Uncle Ted. His hands fall from his face. 'Oh, Jesus Christ.'

'We didn't want to say until we knew what would happen with Thomas,' says Adam. 'But it's all right, isn't it? It will be all right?'

He asks it of me, but it's Ted who replies. 'Move into the big house,' he says. 'Keep as quiet as you can. Don't go anywhere alone and keep those lumps hidden.' The fear in his voice is like the charge in the air before a lightning storm.

'They'll come around,' I say.

'No. No, they won't.' And with that he leaves the circle too.

The knife has fallen and we are split. With the death of our doctor, there is no way to heal this wound.

\* \* \*

It's raining. The cold has seeped into everything. We all complain of it, but I think maybe we are really complaining about our fear. It is the same feeling—icy fingers around us, squeezing, as the silence stretches on from the other side. Those we once recognised as part of us will break it all, just as winter breaks the world down into death.

We sit in the large room where Uncle Ted once threatened me. That feels like a very long time ago. The table has been pushed back against the wall, and blankets and cushions cover the floor.

The teenagers like this room. The tall windows let in the sun, if there is any to see. Not today, though. This is the slowest Sunday I can remember. I've told all my old stories so many times over the past weeks, and there are no new ones in me. I hoped Holly might inspire me, but she is a clean sheet of paper. Even her cries do not move me. They sound automatic, like the cheeping of a bird for its mother. Mindless. This scares me too, and adds to the cold.

Thankfully, Holly sleeps a lot in Thomas's arms. Thomas has commandeered a corner of this room, and it's rare that he moves from it. He keeps blankets piled high around him, covering his body and the baby. He smells terrible. Betty is the only one who does not seem to mind. It stands near to him, unmoving. I've not seen it touch him or the baby. I don't even hear it hum.

The cooking duties have fallen to Adam and Paul, to keep them out of mischief during their own swellings. Alas, their cooking is terrible! They take the dried ingredients we have left and serve up lumpy stews and leaky grey omelettes, which Thomas eats with gusto. He's the only one.

It can't be past two in the afternoon, but already it's getting difficult to discern any edges to the room. Is Thomas asleep again? He doesn't move as I stand and stretch out my legs. Uncle Ted is out. I don't ask where he goes. The others are doing chores, or at least watching their Beauties do the chores for them. All of the manual tasks have been taken away now and our muscles are dissipating, leaving us with weakening arms. We have become reliant.

'Want to hold her?' says Thomas. So he is awake after all, looking at me with the hope of kindness in his eyes. It occurs to me that his new role might not give him everything he needs. There is loneliness, fear and even guilt in such heavy responsibilities. And he is the first to feel these things. Thomas never did like to go first, even in the classroom.

I walk over to him. Bee does not bother to follow. It has stopped sharing with me lately and does not show me visions. Or maybe I stopped sharing with it. I don't know which. All I'm sure of is that I often find myself checking my hip for signs of a lump and feel such relief when there is nothing to be found.

'All right then,' I say. The smell is awful, like curdled milk. He throws back the top blanket and Holly is there, crinkled yellow skin, sticky brown hair in clumps and a face like a painting, not quite human, yet too human to be real.

Thomas holds out his arms. The image of Betty taking off Doctor Ben's head comes into my mind. I say, 'No, I'll just watch her.'

'Okay.' Is it my imagination or does he seem relieved at that? He wets his lips with his tongue, and says, 'I don't really like to let her go, and Betty can feel it.'

'Of course.'

'But if you wanted to hold her, then I'm sure—'

'No. It's fine.'

He looks around the empty room. 'Everything has changed, hasn't it? I wouldn't say this in front of the others, but it's not what you promised.'

'Later,' I say. 'It all comes good later. When has there ever been a bumper crop without a harsh winter? Maybe we don't get the benefit of this harvest, but Holly does. I didn't understand before.' I still don't understand now, but he needs something to imagine, and I'll give him a long straight road in his head that leads to better times. I don't have to believe it to make him see it; I've learned that now.

I talk and talk about Holly's life-in-waiting, and he laps it up. It'll be like before, I tell him. She will be the mother of new women, and humans and Beauty will live in harmony. The Beauty will be our benevolent guardians, stopping us from listening to the worst things in our hearts, making everything perfect this time around. Maybe there will be cities again, but with no crime, no pain; harmony in form and intent. And what will it matter if some of us are pink-skinned, and some of us are brown and some of us are yellow? We'll overcome such unimportant matters.

I could go on forever, spinning this new world of tall towers and hand-holding, but Holly is opening and closing her mouth, wriggling in her blanket. No sound comes out, but I feel her hunger. She transmits it. I've never felt something so clearly from a Beauty, even from Bee. It's intense and painful. Unwelcome.

'She's hungry.' Thomas hesitates, his body curved over her.

'You want me to get some milk from the kitchen?' I ask him.

'Listen, I've not been giving her milk.' He swallows. 'Please don't freak out if I show you this.' He takes off more blankets and reveals his familiar fat pale body; I've seen it many times. I expected a long red scar where Holly pushed her way through—but the skin looks clean and whole, apart from one puckered red mole on his hip.

He manoeuvres Holly to the mole. Her mouth puckers. The mole expands in response to her need. It opens, uncurling, the edges pulling backwards, and inside is a moist purplish hole that begins to weep a white liquid.

Holly's head cranes forward—I didn't know she had such strength already—and she latches on, her lips fitting around the folds. Thomas shudders and his eyelids flutter.

'It feels good,' he whispers.

To watch this makes me feel wrong inside, like nothing has before, even death. That blind expression of pleasure on both their faces, and the sucking sound; I am repulsed and excited. It sickens me and attracts me and my body responds to the idea of it, even as my mind tells me it is horrible, horrible.

I don't move. I watch Thomas feed his baby.

He opens his eyes and says softly, as she feeds, 'Are you disgusted? I am, sometimes. Do you know what's even worse? Betty uses this new hole too. When we… Betty has a long thin yellow tube that comes out of it. Between its legs. And it puts that in there. It feels like nothing I've ever felt before. So good. I couldn't stop it. I don't want to. It's like when I come with my cock, but ten times stronger. And longer. It lasts for minutes.'

'Don't tell the others,' I say.

'Not even Adam and Paul?' he asks.

'No. Let them come to it on their own. Like you did.'

'Yes, maybe that'll be better.'

If the other side found out, William and Eamon and the others, they'd find a way to kill Thomas and Holly, for sure. And the teenagers. They'd find a way, or they'd die trying.

'I guess it's a good thing I'm not using my cock for it any more,' Thomas says, with a shrug that makes the baby grumble against his hip. 'Look.' He flips back the final blanket. At first I see only a hairless flap of skin, like the medical books said a woman should have, but then I see the stub of his cock, no more than a nub. There are no balls in the remains of the pouch beneath. 'I use it to piss with and that's it. No feeling in it.'

'None?' I ask.

'Just enough to tell me where I'm aiming.' He smiles, but I can't make my face mirror his. 'It doesn't hurt,' he says. 'None of it does, now. Having Holly; that was the worst pain I've ever felt. Maybe that's why all of this seems so petty now. Who cares where the milk comes out of? She has to be fed. Doesn't she?'

'Don't tell anyone,' I say. 'Not anyone. For Holly's sake.'

'I won't. Besides, Betty will protect me. And all the babies, when they come. I wonder if you'll have a baby. I didn't think—it makes you complete, Nate. In a way I can't explain.'

Holly keeps feeding. Thomas pulls the blankets back around them both and I am glad not to have to look at his changing body any more. He is like a fattening caterpillar. I can't bear to think of what is happening inside him to make him a producer of babies, of milk. And yet he remains Thomas. I don't understand how he can be Thomas and a mother and a caterpillar, all at the same time.

Behind us, there is a sound.

I turn around smartly and see Bee moving to the door. It leaves without waiting for me, without hesitation. Betty remains still, beside Thomas.

'What?' he says.

'I don't know. Stay here.'

By the time I've reached the front door I can hear the shouting. William's voice is as loud as I've ever heard it; I scramble to the campfire, shoeless, feeling the bite of the icy ground under my feet. William's strident voice becomes distinguishable words. He says, '…must be done. Stay back, we're making the rules…'

…and I see the men who wait outside William's house.

On the ground there are two beheaded bodies of the Beauty, leaking yellow-grey liquid from the stumps of their necks. The other Beauties have formed a line, Bee in the centre, walking slowly towards the house.

The men hold out hoes, shovels, knives: weapons that jut from their readied hands, making the sharp shapes of battle. Hal and Gareth are as tall as pillars and sitting between them, underneath the bell, are Adam and Paul, their faces the colour of paper.

William shouts: 'It must be done, for the sake of us all. We have ruled that it's a crime to put such things in us against our will.' Are his words directed at the Beauty? They walk on, showing no sign of stopping, and William's voice pours on in a scream. I see it like a ribbon spooling from his mouth: 'Judgement has been passed, and now must be carried out, do it, do it—'

Hal and Gareth raise their long knives and swing them, down and round, into the sides of Adam and Paul. The knives stick in the bumps. I see Hal and Gareth working to tug the blades free and Adam and Paul's blood is like glue on the knives, their bodies moulding to the blades, and red and yellow intermingle while their arms and legs and heads twitch. They slump down dead in deference to the knives, the knives are the masters of the body now. And yet the blades won't come free. Hal and Gareth tug, tug, tug, and the knives don't work free.

The Beauty reach them. They start to pull Hal and Gareth apart, beginning with the heads, which are twisted round and popped off. Then the arms, then the legs. The knives are forgotten. There is blood as copious as a river after rainfall. It soaks and sprays William's porch like the painting of a child who can't resist the thrill of the deep rich red.

The Beauty go on, moving through the other men. I see William disassembled, and Eamon, and Landers and Keith D and other men I have known so well. Some of them run for the woods, and some even make it, but a few of the Beauty peel off in the shape of an arrow and follow to the trees, in silence, with certainty.

The other teenagers, Jason and Oliver, come out of the orchard. They stand stock-still, their faces a picture of terror. I think, if I am to describe this day, I must remember their faces, and so I fix the stretched cheeks, the peeled-back lips, in my mind. Then I touch my face and realise I am making the same expression.

Jason and Oliver stumble away into the woods. I am alone.

I reach for Bee with my mind and feel nothing. There is the sound of wailing amidst the trees. It goes on and on. It's surely not a human sound. The Beauty must be making it. I listen to it, waiting for it to stop, for something to happen. Maybe Uncle Ted will appear and start to issue commands, clean up that mess, bury those bodies. But there's nothing. Just the ceaseless wailing.

Eventually the cold penetrates my feet, and brings me to the knowledge that I must move. So I do. I return to Thomas, who sits in the room just as I left him, Holly in his lap, his eyes closed.

'No,' he says. 'Don't. I can't hear it. I can't hear it.' His voice shoots up, spiralling into shrill denial.

But I must speak. I say, 'They're dead.'

Thomas says, 'No.' When he opens his eyes, they are alive with confusion and dread. 'Don't let them hurt her.'

'Nobody will. They're all dead. The Beauty killed them all.'

'All of them?' The worst thing is the hope in his face. Holly is more important than the rest of us, to him. 'The whole Group? William? Everyone?'

'Some ran. The Beauty have gone after them.'

'Everyone,' he says. Then he adds, 'I'm very tired.'

'Me too,' I whisper.

I can hear the wailing of the Beauty through the window. I crawl up next to Thomas and Holly, and I make us into a protective pile. I need an answer, a different ending to this story.

An answer must come to me.

* * *

The icy depths of the graveyard remain undisturbed come the morning. The frozen cobwebs hang in tatters from the bare branches and the Beauty bury their dead lovers elsewhere, out of sight. In the woods, I think. With the bodies of the women that Uncle Ted strangled once upon a time, to protect us. The things that get done in the name of protection.

Maybe new Beauties will erupt from the fresh corpses. Is this a circle, a journey in which we come back to the beginning and feel so much more complete in our knowledge? I'm losing my taste for such easy words.

I sit next to my mother's grave. Bee stands outside, silent. I am never truly alone now. Bee will always pull on my senses and I would give my voice, all my stories, to go back to how things were. Loneliness—that was a rare gift, like a hole in the brain that I worked hard to fill with my thoughts. Now I no longer have a hole to fill, and so I do not think so much. I only feel. How I hate such feelings.

My mother would flick through her glossy magazines and sigh. 'We never appreciate what we have until it's gone,' she would say, and I used to think in my head, never out loud, that it wasn't too late. If she wanted that life so badly she could go back. How little I understood.

I put a hand on the cold wooden cross that marks her spot. It's not that different from touching Bee.

A voice says, 'I thought I'd find you here.'

Ahh, the relief I feel in hearing that voice! I can't help it; I spring up, I go to Uncle Ted and I put my arms around him. He has a smell so familiar that I close my eyes and imagine myself young again, young enough to be swung up into the space between his arms where happiness lives. But when I open my eyes I see his Bonnie standing next to my Bee and I step back. I pick up my problems once more, and own them.

I say, 'I thought you were dead.'

He says, 'They knew I was no threat. I hid in the woods. I know them well enough to keep out the way when it's needed, and to come out when trouble passes. I wish I could say the same of you. You can't hide in here all day. There's work to be done. I've called an emergency meeting.'

I laugh. I didn't know I could make such a sound again. The graveyard soaks it up. 'A meeting?' I say. 'Did you not see what happened? Who do you think is going to show up?'

'Typical overblown Nate. You're alive. I'm alive. Thomas and that thing he calls a baby, and Oliver and Jason. No doubt more of these bastard crosses will start growing inside all of you soon, and if we want them to be more human than mushroom then we need to have order. Agreement.'

'And you,' I say. 'A baby will probably grow in you too.'

I see the flare of disgust on his face. He steps back and rests his hand on the stick on his belt. 'That's not going to happen,' he tells me, and Bonnie makes a strange wail. Then I understand—the way he makes Bonnie keep its distance, walk behind him, never touch him. This is not only in public. He does not touch it at all. I can't imagine the strength of will this must take, or what it might do to a man. I wonder if it isn't sending him crazy.

'How can you—'

He cuts me off. 'Meeting. Now. In the kitchen. There aren't any answers in here, Nate.'

'I know.'

There are no answers anywhere in this place. Not in the graveyard, the kitchen, the vegetable patch, the orchard, the clearing or the clifftop. Ted will try to inject us with meaning, but it cannot be done. At least, not the meaning he wants. I wait until he is gone, and then I lean over and am sick next to my mother's grave. The vomit is stringy and yellow. It tastes of mushrooms.

\* \* \*

The kitchen is warm, and comforting. It would be easy to imagine nothing has changed.

I've not had much to do with Jason and Oliver before. They are still young, training to be carpenters and woodsmen, and the life of an apprentice is a busy one. I saw them at the campfire and my eyes would skim over them as I told my stories, but the truth was I considered myself to be above them and I did not bother to make friends.

I see now that this was a mistake. They know Ted well and they are loyal to him, in the way that men of manual labour are. They trust others who work with their hands and think those of the mind are sly and consider themselves above others. What can I say? They are right. So now I have no ally but Thomas, who hears nothing I say any more unless I put the word 'baby' in the sentence.

'All the hard tasks have been taken over by the Beauty,' says Ted, leaning back against the stove, a position of power. 'So we only have to cook for ourselves from our supplies and raise Holly right. These are our tasks now.'

I notice he does not mention the idea of other babies to Oliver and Jason. They stand close together in front of the pantry door. Thomas has been cajoled into having a wash and getting dressed. He wears a woollen dress and holds Holly to his chest, jiggling her up and down while she makes small mews of discomfort, projecting her need for Betty who has been left outside with the other Beauties.

I wonder if the others do not feel her pain. From her mind she pushes forth a feeling, her desire for a figure that can only be described as *father*. She sees Betty as her father.

Jason raises a hand. He has a smooth, pleasant face, without the scars of acne that one might expect at his age, and he wears a red band in his long brown hair. 'So are we all cooks now?' he says.

Thomas jerks up his head, and Ted says smoothly, 'Thomas remains the lead cook. The rest of us will listen to him in this department. And we can start to plan for the future. When Holly gets old enough, there will be lessons to teach. A future to plan for.'

This must be the reason he has not simply left us and gone off into his beloved woods for good. I picture Holly as a toddler, a child, a woman. Other children to follow. Yes, Ted has the future of all mankind in his sights, the continuation of the race, bred back to humanity. If the Beauty have different plans for Holly, what will we do?

I don't want to think on his plans, his battles. I feel sick, so sick. I want to crawl away and never speak again. But that is not the fate Ted has plotted out for me.

He says, 'Nate, you remain the storyteller. You speak of our past. There are so many to remember now. William, Eamon, everyone who has fallen. And the women, of course. You must still speak of the women.'

The others murmur agreement as I shake my head. I say, 'I can't. I've lost the taste for it.'

'You think this is about your taste?' says Ted. He speaks slow and soft, his narrowed eyes on me. 'This is about those who died for you, and we will remember them. You will make their sacrifices worthwhile, and in their memory we will find the strength to go on. Can you not agree that it is the only fair and just thing to do?'

He has me and he knows it. Even Thomas will not side with me; he loves his stories too much.

I don't reply. Ted takes it as assent so he forges onwards like a machine, with his blunt, brutal words. He has no skill at this. He is not weaving a world with his words. He is only smashing down on us, hammering on our heads. Ted says, 'We must go on. We must take care of Holly and each other. That is all we have now.'

I hold my tongue as he looks around the kitchen and then drops his eyes. The meeting is over. Jason moves to the kitchen door and opens it to admit our Beauties, then yelps in surprise. I look past him, to the yellow yellow yellow in the corridor, filling the space. All of the Beauty, and more besides, back from hiding the dead, are squashing into each other, all of their blank faces turned to us. I sense a wave of longing, of expectation that is so strong, so very strong.

'What are they doing?' says Ted. I hear fear in his voice and that is terrible, worse than when he is fearless.

Thomas pushes forward, Holly held out in his arms. 'Get

out!' he squawks at the crowd of Beauty. 'You'll hurt the baby!' And that works. The tide is turned. They shrink back, still facing us, but their need is a terrible thing to feel. It is a force that they can barely control in themselves. They want love. Their partners are dead and they all want to be loved.

'Come on,' Thomas says, and we move behind him, down the corridor, to the open front door. The Beauty fall back to the outside. Only the ones to which we are bonded remain with us—I feel Bee's strength beside me. It helps Thomas and I to close the door upon the others. The loneliness they exert is giving me a headache.

Once they are locked out, I run to the dining room window and look upon them as a sea of longing.

Bee touches me gently on the shoulders, and I feel its determination to keep me safe. It puts one hand on my left hip, upon the small lump that has grown there. It thinks of love and of family. How human it is becoming.

I do not shy away from Bee's embrace. I let it hold me and take comfort, while there is still comfort to take.

# PART
# FOUR

Thomas plants runner bean seedlings. He grows them on the kitchen windowsill where they can enjoy the sparing sun of early spring and the residual heat of the stove. Holly is wrapped up close to his heart, in a length of green curtain that he took from one of the bedrooms we no longer use. We all sleep in the dining room now, pressed down deep together while the Unloved hum outside the walls.

I hold Thomas's watering can for him. He swaps it for his small spade at the end of every row so he can welcome his thirsty little shoots to the garden. He murmurs to himself, or maybe to the plants. He does love runner beans so.

I love them too. At least, I love these ones looking so questing and perky. Spring has come around with a determination that has taken all of us by surprise. I had thought it would sneak in, ashamed to be seen in this place, but no! The snowdrops will trumpet and the birds will shout. Change comes. Doesn't it always? Then why am I so grateful for it?

Our Beauties live in the house with us and have become very different from the Unloved. They are also seedlings, I see now, just beginning to bud with personalities of their own. I could always tell Bee apart, but now I know all the ones to which we bonded.

Jason's Bernadette is the most active and cannot stand still for long without giving strange little hops, rather like a dance to the personal music in its head. Bonnie is the opposite—so still. I realise now it enjoys being subservient to Uncle Ted. It fetches and carries and stands in his shadow, with such quiet pride. Oliver has his Bess, to whom he always looks so many times throughout the day, as if it makes all decisions for him.

Betty remains devoted to Thomas and Holly, but is stern in its love, rather removed. It stands over them at all times; right now, it is in the shade of the red brick wall with Thomas's sun hat on its head for some reason. I know its severe personality well enough to find this a comical juxtaposition, and Bee is emitting a bubbling hum that tells me it finds this funny too.

'Can,' says Thomas. I take his spade and give him the can.

There are moments, comic pauses, every day amidst our dread. Another surprise. Months have passed since William and the others were killed and the Beauty split, just as our Group split, to create the Unloved. Bee and the others guard us, but the Unloved want in. They want it with a passion that seeps through brick and glass. They stand and hum all day and all night. I think the only reason they do not come in is the fact that I am pregnant and Holly is so small. The offspring are of the greatest concern. But this will surely not last forever.

'I'm telling a special story tonight,' I say to Thomas's back, as he waters his seedlings. I've thought this through so carefully. Ted is powerless—what can he do to me? We are all prisoners in this house now and this captivity has given me back my voice. There is one more story that I must tell.

'Spade,' says Thomas. I take the can and give him back his spade.

The Unloved hum on. I could almost pretend, in this gift

of bright morning sunshine, that this is midsummer and the hum outside the walls is only the heavy drone of bees.

But I will have a baby of my own by then and will have no time for sunbathing. I will feed my baby from a hole in my hip, and my cock and balls will shrivel away to nothing. The idea of this was worse when it was happening to someone else. Now it is me and it is inevitable, and nothing inevitable is ever that bad. If I have to live with it, then how can it be unbearable?

Besides, bodies betray us. That is what they do. They die and this is, at least, not death. I will choose any option but death. This body wants the story to go on.

'Thomas,' I say. 'This can't end well.'

He says, 'Hmph.'

'The babies will only be young for so long.'

'So we'll have more.'

He understands this breeding, growing, training. It's part of the garden too.

'I reckon,' he says, 'that the Unloved will give up and go away. Look for other men to bond with. Beyond the rocks, back down to the town.'

'You think the town is still there?' I ask him.

'Why wouldn't it be?'

He has spoken of the thing that has obsessed me over these long nights. It used to be that the Group and the Valley of the Rocks was everything to me. But this, too, is changing.

I say, 'We should go look.'

Thomas says, 'What?'

'Find other men. Bring them back here for the Unloved. Then they'll leave us alone.'

He says, 'Just stroll out through the front door? You first.' He digs fast and dirt sprays up from his spade. There are only a few seedlings left to be planted.

'We can go. With a baby in me and Holly against your chest, they won't touch us.'

'So you say.' He throws a look over his shoulder and in it I see he has finally grown up and away from me. I am no longer the leader between us two. Now he is in charge because he has Holly. He has travelled to this new place first and I must be the one to follow.

'The Unloved won't be able to stop themselves for much longer,' I say. 'They will come in and they will kill the Beauty, and then they will take us and use us. Maybe they'll even kill the babies so they can make their own with us. The Beauty and the Unloved grow apart every day. Soon they won't recognise each other at all.'

Thomas stands up abruptly. Holly whines against his chest and Betty takes a half-step forward.

He says, 'What's happened to your stories of forever rainbows and lullabies? You want to tell horror tales now it suits your purpose? You can tell those someplace else. I've got no interest in listening. If you haven't noticed, Nate, there are children to think about now. I need to hear a better future than the one you've chosen to tell. For Holly's sake, and for the sake of the baby inside you, you need to stick to the old stories. You owe it to them, if not to me. You owe it to them!'

'You don't believe they need to hear the truth?' I ask.

I don't know what happens. There is an intense pain in my temple, like the sting of a hundred wasps—I clap my hands to it, feel the wetness of blood. Then I see the spade on the ground, near my feet. Thomas threw it. He threw it straight at me. His face is grey with shock.

Bee moves forward, so fast, and Betty is moving too—

'No!' I say. 'No! I'm fine. I'm fine. It's not serious.' I spread my hands, show the blood on my fingers. It isn't a lot. I feel a trickle down my cheek. 'I swear it's not serious.'

Bee and Betty stop coming towards us. Betty still wears that ridiculous sun hat. My head throbs in the sun. I will have a terrible headache, but that is nothing new. I've had a headache for months from the thoughts, the desires and the rages of the Unloved. But I am alive. We are all still alive.

Thomas opens his mouth. He shuts it. He bends down and retrieves his spade. Holly's wails grow into sharp cries.

'You know I'm right,' I tell him.

'Holly wants feeding,' he says, and he goes inside. Betty follows.

I plant the final seedlings with my hands, and then water them.

\* \* \*

*To start—*

*There was only one. Then one divided into two, and two into four, and on it went, each division bringing a new reality, a new possibility. Sometimes the many that sprang from the one agreed and moved with a mutual purpose. And sometimes they didn't.*

*It's an impossibility to calculate when the many became too many. Things are born and they die. They bleed and divide and begin again. But in one moment they changed from living in a land of plenty to lacking the one thing they needed above all others.*

*Love.*

*They lacked love. And the lack of love, new questions— questions that had not been asked before—came into their minds. Why should some have happiness and others have none? Such thoughts lead to jealousy, and that alters you inside. You lose sense of the paths, the divisions that you can walk, and you see just one road, long and grey and loveless.*

*And so the Beauty divided again. They became the Beauty and the Unloved, and there was no return from that division.*

*The Unloved no longer recognised the Beauty as part of them. Instead they waited for the chance to take the love away from the Beauty. They wanted their own future, for that is what all living things want, and they could not be blamed for that. But they forgot how to be gentle, to be reasonable. They had started down a path that could only lead to death.*

*Or could it?*

*It's important to remember that there have always been such divisions. That is the basis of life. Division brings not only discord, but also hope. Who knows what will happen when the rules ceaselessly change? Those that were weak may grow strong. Those that are strong may lose themselves and fall away. And those that once upon a time did not dare to act, may yet find the strength to take the road that reaches into places that nobody else will dare to go.*

*The past, the present and the future—none of those are set. We know that now. They change as we change.*

*So let us write a new ending to our story.*

*Let us say—the Unloved waited for the chance to take the love away from the Beauty. Every day their patience got a little less, and their desire grew a little more. It is so very difficult to be alone when others are not.*

*Then one day they could take it no longer. And they became one again, united in their pain. They acted as one, surging towards the house with plans to murder the Beauty and find happiness in the flesh of the men they found inside. They threw their weight against the doors, the windows, the walls—and the house started to creak, to groan, while the men inside wept with fear. The house could not keep them safe. It would fall.*

*And then, from the road that led out of the Valley of the Rocks, a sound: singing. Men singing, a mass of men, men who had known and lived in loneliness too since their women died so long ago. The men poured into the Valley, their voices loud, their arms open, and there was a man for every Unloved.*

*Leading the men to their destiny were Nate and Thomas, brave ones, with babies of their own in their arms and a future to fight for. They had gone out into the world and found that future, and brought it back to the Valley. And so the Group could begin again, the many becoming one, the one growing and growing, to make a beautiful world populated with so many happy men, on and on, until the end.*

* * *

'No,' says Thomas.

The dining room is lit only by a few candles and the smouldering logs in the grate. He stands up and he is alive with his indignation; it jumps out of him like the short, sharp breaths he exhales.

I try to tell him with my eyes that I am sorry, but it must be done. I must get Ted to side with me, to order us away. It's our only chance. 'We'll go and get help. We'll save everyone. You'll be a hero,' I tell him.

'No. Not now. Not ever.' The candlelight makes him look bigger, taller. He has a dignity that I have not seen in him before. Thomas says, 'You say the Unloved will kill and rape, and I say they won't. Why are you right, and I am wrong? Just because you know how to wrap it up in a story?' He is warming to his outrage, his hands flying out like sparks. The curtain wrapped around his chest where Holly rests gives him the air of invincibility.

Ted stays in his chair, arms crossed, not bothering to stir himself. Bonnie stands to attention behind him. 'Nate,' he says, with a smile, 'what makes you so sure that the Unloved, as you have named them, want us? Perhaps they are simply protecting the children. In which case, they're not going to be happy if you try to take Thomas and Holly away with you. Besides, lad, if they really wanted to come in they could. Windows can be smashed. Doors can be knocked down. They're easily strong enough for that.'

I hate the way he diminishes me with his 'lad'. Oliver and Jason, on blankets near the fire, nod along. I will need better arguments.

I say, 'If they are only protecting us, why are we cowering in the house all day and all night? Why don't you simply walk outside, Uncle Ted? Right now?'

He shrugs. 'What is there to go outside for? We've had a long cold winter and it's been easier to stay indoors. That's all. I think maybe those long dark nights and your... pregnancy... are playing tricks on your brain, lad. Come the summer, everything will look better. We'll go out, into the woods maybe. When your little one arrives, we'll have a fine time playing out together.'

Jason and Oliver have copied Ted's smile. Thomas sits back down with an air of vindication. Can they really not feel it? This threat that encloses the house? Or perhaps they cannot name it. They have no practice in naming the truth and now they do not trust me to do it for them.

I see in the four faces that patronise me that my time as a storyteller is at an end. I have no listeners any more. I could talk on and on and it would be as if the world had gone deaf.

I can't stay here.

'If nobody will come with me, then I'll go myself,' I say. 'I'll save you, even if you don't want saving.'

'Don't be an idiot.' Ted shifts in his seat. He says, 'You and your jumped-up ideas. I always knew it would lead us all into trouble. You need to learn how to give up your selfish ways now. There's that thing in your body to think about. The mushrooms are so desperate to keep it safe and I'm not going to let you put us all in danger.'

'What are you going to do? Keep me here against my will?'

'So melodramatic, as usual. So keen to sniff out a good tale. From now on, I'll tell the tales and you can shut up and listen. You're just like your mother. Get yourself into trouble, and then whine when you're told what to do.' He gets up and faces me; I can see he is what he believes a man should be. His hand moves to the stick in his belt. How he loves to threaten those that are weaker. My mother gave way to him. Maybe I was in her body already when she was brought here and Ted told her it was the only way to be safe from the scary world out there.

Now the same choice is upon me. And I find I am not powerless. Not at all.

'Get back,' I say. 'You are not to touch me.'

Bee shifts from the corner of the room. The other Beauties stir, rock from side to side.

'I've known you since you were a baby, Nathan, and I will reprimand you if that is necessary. Don't push me, boy.'

I put my hands on my bump. It is cold and firm, getting bigger every day. I say, 'I'm no longer a boy, Uncle Ted. And I will leave this place.'

He says, 'You will not.'

I take a step forward. He blocks my path to the door.

But I am the powerful one. I have the baby in me, and he cannot touch me. He knows it. I see it behind that mask of stone he uses.

He steps aside.

'Nate!' calls Thomas, a plea. I ignore him and carry on walking to the kitchen. I grab a canvas bag from under the sink and take it to the larder. It's too dark to see properly. I grab whatever I can identify: some stored apples, some bread.

The larder door slams behind me. The darkness is total. I yelp, sounding like a dog. It takes me an age of groping to find the handle, but my relief gives way to intense dread when the handle won't turn. It won't move for me. I am trapped.

'Stay in there until you learn some sense,' says Ted, from the other side.

This is what Ted does. He forces his problems into the dark, and keeps them there. Like my mother's feelings, like the women he killed and buried in the forest. But I will not be kept in the dark. He has finally managed to teach me how to be a man. I will do whatever is necessary to beat him. I am ready to kill.

I call Bee with my mind. I tell it what to do. I show it a picture, every detail, with slow deliberation. I leave nothing out.

Then I wait.

I hear Thomas and Ted arguing, but I pay no attention. I concentrate on what Bee shows me. I can see through Bee's eyes.

Bee is coming, moving to the kitchen. It shows me that Ted has jammed his chair against the pantry door and is sitting on it. Thomas, Jason and Oliver hover, trying to persuade him to move. Are those tears on Thomas's cheeks?

Bee touches nobody but Ted. It picks him up by his neck. I thrill at the strength of my beautiful Bee. Ted does not make a sound, but he fights and fights, his kicks and punches connecting. Bee feels arms around the waist. Bonnie is in the room, squeezing hard, fighting for Ted. I feel white pain in my mind, but Bonnie is not strong enough to stop this. Bee knocks Bonnie down, and looks around.

The others huddle back against the sink. Holly is awake now, I feel her fear. She wails. The Unloved hum, hum, hum—a nest of hornets. Bright red flowers in my head light up my darkness. But I tell Bee—do it. Do it.

Bee grabs one of Ted's arms as he flails and breaks it, clean, like the snapping of a stick. He goes limp. Bee carries Ted out of the kitchen, down the corridor to the front door. It opens the door, and throws him out into the night.

Bonnie screams. It is a human sound. It plunges out after Ted, and Bee closes the door, not looking at what is happening. It does not want to look.

The larder door opens and my normal vision returns. I can see Thomas's tear-soaked face. He holds out his arms to me and I push past him and go to Bee. I let it scoop me up and hold me tight. It pats the bump, over and over. I feel our mutual relief amplified in my mind like a circle, no beginning, no end.

Outside, Bonnie screams and screams. When it stops we can hear Ted's pleading. He begs and moans and demands that they stop, but the Unloved continue to hum with an expressive and endless happiness.

*   *   *

In the morning, they are gone. Ted too. Perhaps into the woods, I don't know. Bee doesn't either. It has lost all connection to them, but it thinks they have gone for good.

All that is left are the scattered yellow and grey lumps that were once Bonnie.

\* \* \*

I stand outside where the Group once made its campfire. It's a chilly spring morning, but bright. The grass is growing back over that burned circle of earth. Thomas, Jason and Oliver stand close together, looking around like baby birds seeing out of the nest for the first time. How small our lives have become.

I heave the canvas bag over my shoulder.

'Well then,' I say. 'Goodbye.'

'Don't go,' says Jason. Oliver bursts into tears and his Bess reaches out to him, then wraps him up in its love.

'What do you want?' says Thomas. He has Holly out of the curtain papoose for once, in the crook of his arm. She is looking around with wide grey eyes and her skin is a very pale yellow. She is as beautiful as the daffodils that are starting to poke through the remains of William's house, and as natural to behold. It is undeniable that she deserves her place in the world.

I say, 'Nothing. Only to go. That's all there is, now.'

He says, 'You want me to say I'm sorry? Because I am. If you were a true friend you would forgive me, and forget all this nonsense.'

'I do forgive you.'

'Then stay. We need you. You have to tell us what to do. Please, Nate. Stay.'

I don't answer. I'm sick of words. Instead, I show Bee a picture in my mind: the two of us together, our baby inside me, walking out of this place. Going to find out what remains of humanity. Not to bring anything back, not even to find new stories to tell. Just for the sake of knowing.

Bee agrees. It holds out a hand and I take it. We start to walk, following the path that leads out of the Valley of the Rocks. It is a path that unravels one step at a time, on and on, with no end.

## ACKNOWLEDGEMENTS

Thanks to John Griffiths, Tim Stretton, and everyone at UKAuthors for continuing to read the things I write.

I have lots of ongoing gratitude for Neil Ayres and Francesca Kemp. You make my daily emails worth reading and keep me moving in the right direction. Thank you with bells on.

Anne Zanoni put her skill and hard work into this book, and I'm so glad she did. Thanks Anne. And George Sandison read it, liked it, and published it. For that, and for the dedication he has put into making it the best it can be, he deserves more than an acknowledgement. George—I owe you a beer. Or an ice cream.

And go Team Whiteley.

READ ON FOR A

# BRAND-NEW SHORT STORY

by

ALIYA
WHITELEY

# PEACE, PIPE

# ONE
# HOME

The word that gets me through the first two days is *home*.

I say it a lot, rhythmically, in time with the splash of water from some sporadically gurgling pipe. The water rushes through the plumbing behind the wall, beside my bed in this windowless, inescapable room, and I say: *home*. The sounds, linked together this way, calm me. They remind me that I will return, and the sun will warm me once more. Three months to wait.

If I had a family, I would probably say their names instead, but I've never been good at attachments. I am without such names to say, and so I say *home*.

Earth is not such a satisfying word, so I don't say that. It's the long, mournful 'o' that I need, and besides, when I think of Earth generally it's for business purposes—a destination, a departure point, and an eventual arrival. It's a full time job being an Earth person. And missing the sun, well, that's not quite the same as missing the Earth, to my mind.

I have a house. It's in a decent gated community. I rented it out to a couple. An agency manages the letting, and they send regular mails to reassure me about the state of the property. I'm glad to know everything is fine, but still, I don't miss the house either.

On the third day of repeating *home* I realise that I'm not thinking at all when I say the word. I'm feeling. Or, at least, constructing an approximation of a feeling, of how I might feel when I get home. If I ever do. Because it seems to me I've never been there yet.

*Home.*

The pipe behind the wall gurgles, and I say it again. *Home.* It becomes a pattern, then a superstition. It comforts me.

I begin to credit the pipe with thoughts of its own.

I can't banish the idea that an intelligent pipe is gurgling, and waiting for my response. The superstition lies on both sides of the wall. It might suspect that I am a boring automatic noise from some machine. *Home* I say, and the pipe thinks, *there it is, right on cue, that machine. How comforting. Or could it be alive?*

It takes courage to break a superstition. I'm not usually bothered about such things; it just goes to show how circumstance can alter personality in such a short time. Admittedly, I carried a coin on me at all times. A penny. Pennies are lucky, aren't they? Mine bore the likeness of a King. I found it on the street before I took my final practical exam for Group F. Unbelievable, I know—a rare and beautiful find, just at the white-pillared entrance to the main building. Probably dropped by some important person, and their loss was my gain. I passed the exam, and it became an omen of success that then travelled with me. But everything was taken away after the arrival at quarantine. I don't cry, but if I'd been that sort of person I might have wept for that coin.

So I have felt emotions for an inanimate object before, as well as for all the creatures of the universe that I have greeted. I'll talk to the pipe to pass the time; that's fine. Am I losing my mind? I could take up the offer of a psychiatrist but what would I say? I am afraid of what I might say, such as:

I killed them.

No, I condemned them. It is not the same thing. I have

instigated a chain of events that will kill them. Maybe all of them.

It was not a long flight back but it was without contact of any kind, conducted entirely on autopilot, and by the time I arrived and the pod was connected directly to the quarantine facility I was not myself any more. I don't know who I was. A person that shouted, and demanded, and begged for knowledge. What was happening on Demeter? I had emotions that could not be controlled, at first. I have never felt such things. There are not even words for them.

But then.

But then I came back to myself. I swallowed the feelings. Every time they rose up within me I swallowed them down. And now I am myself again. Whatever that is, that's what I am. I am a person who wants to go home.

Besides, I find I want to embrace this irrational part of myself. It's a great distraction from what is happening on Demeter. From what I have done.

The first task is to ascertain if the pipe is interested in my response.

*Shoush* says the pipe, and I take a breath in, and hold it.

The pipe and I share a moment. It's a pause, a hush, a surprisingly satisfying minute of mutual awareness. The pipe is waiting for me, and I am not following. *Where is it? The pipe thinks. Where has it gone?* This is off-grid—a new planet, unfamiliar and exciting.

The pipe says again, *Shoush.*

I think it's rattled. Then, quietly, far more quickly than before, it says *shoush?*

An upward inflexion? Seriously? Now we are surely in the realms of my imagination. Could a pipe ever be so obvious? *Shoush?* Again. It gets louder. *Shoush?*

It's not exactly a pipe in my mind any more. It has a mouth. It makes sounds with something like a mouth.

*Shoush*, I say, trying to get the sound right, like the rushing of water. The vibration tickles the back of my throat. It's not even a close approximation of the depth of sound the pipe gets. I try again. *Shoush.*

*Shoush*, it replies.

It's alive. It's alive, and making a word. What word is it making? Perhaps it's a name. It's repeating its own name.

But then I think of myself, sitting in this small room, waiting out my quarantine, talking just to hear the sound of my own voice and to be reminded of the place where I cannot be.

*Home*, I say. *Shoush. Home.*

And then the pipe says something new. It says

*Home.*

# TWO
# GOOD

I've always been good with languages, but that's not exactly my trade. Online I, and others like me, get called Mouthpieces, which is a far from accurate description. I'm a communicator, and a negotiator. As soon as humanity started to explore the planets, we realised one thing: anything warm-blooded that develops in an Earth-like climate follows Darwinist principles. Dog eat dog, alien eat alien. Communication is a huge part of that. Language is an expression of the body—any sort of body—as much as it is a product of higher thought. It's not what you say, it's the way that you say it.

I look at planetary dynamics, observe, and then report back. When you find a brand-new ecosystem, how do you know who to speak to first, who to introduce yourself to, who to do a deal with? Just because something talks doesn't mean it's in charge—it's only Earth, uniquely, that has that distinction. Almost every other planet we've found contains different species sharing a language. It's a survival mechanism. I have a theory about this; a creature that cries out, 'No, please, stop,' is generally harder to eat, I'd imagine.

Once I've established which creatures can be dealt with for trade purposes, and which are unimportant, I write my report. Often I phrase it in Earth equivalencies, for ease of understanding. These are insects, and these are tigers. These are dodos. These are humans, as close as you can get.

Which, of course, deserves a great big 'dangerous' marker on the report.

In the past I have insisted on visiting these planets, and even negotiated trade deals myself, because I am an idiot.

I had thought I'd come across it all, but Pipe is new to me. It learns fast, faster than me, and has quickly learned a variety of English words. It's more intelligent than I am. It makes connections, and seems to understand concepts that I cannot picture, not without seeing it, knowing what it looks like. I keep imagining water when we converse, water with a face. A face that is close to human, of course, with that all-important mouth. How small my imagination is, but that is what experience has taught me to expect.

I could easily research Pipe. A desk with online interface has been activated for me, albeit with access to Demeter files removed for now. I'd start with the term 'water-based life form' and go from there—my paywall rating is pretty good in this area, which is a benefit of the job—but I find I don't want to be told the answers. This mystery of what Pipe is, of what kind of planet it comes from, is the kind of puzzle I enjoy. I have to attempt to overcome the limits of communication. How far can two creatures from different planets take their interaction with no visual contact?

Besides, I have a suspicion that Pipe and I are not meant to be able to hear each other. It could be a fault in the way this vast waypoint in space travel is constructed. It's a sphere, looking something like a much smaller second moon from Earth's perspective, so perhaps the shape allows sound to travel in strange ways. A whispering gallery, even. So maybe Pipe is not on the other side of the wall, but on the other side of this construction. The alternative, however, is that there is a crack between our sealed chambers. My viruses could be sneaking their way through to Pipe, and its tiny nasties could be infecting me right now. When the lights dim to simulate night, I lie in the enforced darkness and feel my skin begin to itch, and I think—this is it. I'll be dead or a puddle by morning. But I'm always here when the lights begin to brighten and the daytime ambience switches on.

If I report hearing noises, will the staff think I'm crazy, or will they uncover a breach, and take me to some new room to start my three months' quarantine all over again? To be honest, I'd rather get Pipe's germs.

*Vurgsh?* I say to Pipe, after breakfast.

It says *vurgsh* back. Then *good.* With a lot of 'o' action. *Goooooooooodsh,* actually, because it can't do harsh sounds well. I can only imagine how mangled my pronunciation sounds to it.

\* \* \*

*Good food?* Pipe asks me. It's amazing how both of our cultures use an upward inflexion for a question; it's the first time I've come across that. It's fascinating.

*Good food,* I confirm. *Vurgsh paps.* I've learned through experience that communication is forwarded at its early stages by lying rather than attempting truthfulness in order to retain the illusion of consistency. The food is not good. It's bran and fruit and toast and juice; how can that be made so untasty? It feels deliberate on the part of the staff. But at least I have a choice. I select options via the online interface every evening, and it arrives in a hermetically sealed bag through the door slot at set mealtimes. If there was no choice the reality of being here would sink in. After all, we can't leave. We just have to pretend that it's what we want to sit here, and then it doesn't sting so much. This is the fifth time I've gone through quarantine, and this time is by far the worst.

I am so grateful for Pipe.

I wonder what prisoners on Pipe's planet eat. Oh no, not *gresh* again, Pipe might be thinking. *Gresh* sounds suitably unappealing. I really should stop making words up, or I'm going to confuse both of us.

*Long. Booooooored*, says Pipe.

*Oh dear*, I say, as a reflex. It uses both words to tell me it's having a bad day, but it seems to use them interchangeably. Perhaps both concepts are the same in its language. *Vah* is the translation.

So many meanings and variations are passing us by.

I wonder if everything long is boring on Planet Pipe. They must all have the attention span of gnats. Quarantine must be so hard on such creatures, and, thinking about it, it makes sense. Doesn't water flow? Isn't it always travelling, moving, making its way over an ever-changing landscape? See, now I'm picturing Pipe as a cross between the Amazon river and a water park. It's huge and free and mighty and carving its way through a continent and also great for entertaining children on hot days.

When we reach the limits of our conversational abilities one of us says *pause*. Usually it's me. There's only so much my brain can take. Then we stop conversing for a little while, and instead I study for an hour or so. My field updates constantly and I'm desperate not to be left behind; there's still so much out there to see, and I have to believe they will let me back out there to see it, even though I know that is probably not true, not after what happened.

Here comes another feeling I must push down deep.

*Pause* can be translated as one drop of water falling—a *plip* sound. It's very difficult to reproduce. Sometimes, after I've attempted it in Pipe language it makes a *ghaauuuuu* sound, which I think is laughter.

That Pipe. What a sense of humour.

# THREE

# BUSY

It's strange to hear yourself being discussed on the news. My life, my colleagues, my mistake. My fault.

The mistake, elevated from social media whisperings to global reporting, is known as Ottercrash. Everybody knows it's a big deal because it has 'crash' on the end. Plus it's a catchy phrase for tagging.

But it wasn't even a crash.

The Otter was the sixth ship I travelled on, the sixth time I was allowed to negotiate a trade deal personally. I loved that ship. I miss it more than I miss the crew, with whom I didn't bond. They were already a close unit, with no room for me, but my room on board the Otter—that was a personal space that welcomed me, was happy to be decorated with my chosen images. I instructed the computer's nervous system to pulse up my favourite photographs along the veins in the walls. They were diverse and deep, to me: orange flowers in a field, the eye of a dragonfly, the bubble complexes seen from space. I included a punkish little otter, the fur on its head upright, spikey, who came with a caption—

*Who are you looking at?*

The crew weren't a bad lot. They really weren't. They were like many groups I've come across—not good with change. My area of expertise is a new science, and I don't think they really took it seriously.

I wish I could say that they ignored my advice, and that's

what led to problems, but that's not what happened. I was clear in my testimony. I missed the signs that I wasn't dealing with the dominant species. Yes, the creatures involved said that they were, but I don't blame them in the circumstances. We made treaties that antagonised the situation, and I was ultimately responsible for starting a war.

See how I frame it in distancing language? I have answered a lot of questions about this already, in front of a panel of Group F representatives via a netlink. But I have never spoken to the media, as per my contract, which is the same thing in the eyes of the watching world as not caring.

I wonder who leaked the situation.

The latest report says:

The war rages on Demeter, with the Beaverin settlements being wiped out in vast numbers by the larger, more aggressive Treeforms who refuse to communicate directly with humanity. The Beaverin, on the other hand, continue to use the equipment left behind in the wreck of the Otter to beg for help. Their cries reach our planet and find us frozen in bureaucracy and debate. The crew of the Otter, representatives of humanity, triggered a catastrophe. The question that cannot be answered, and yet must be asked, is—was this a tragedy that was always going to happen? If we can't sort out the problems of our own planet, shouldn't we leave the rest of the universe well alone?

I find that I'm clenching my fists.

Beaverin and Treeforms are the colloquial descriptions we used in our reports, and they are horrible simplifications of those life forms, and that situation. And Treeforms—if we're going to go with that description—aren't refusing to communicate. It's likely that they communicate a lot. My new theory is that they communicate in an entirely new form that we haven't come across before.

We—I—made the error of thinking that the Treeforms were plants. They look like trees. They don't move around, except in a breeze. They don't make noises. The Beaverin were chewing off their bark and using the materials to make dwellings. My main Beaverin contact—I called him Thumbs, which just goes to show how humanity insists on giving everything stupid names—only came clean about that behaviour later. The Treeforms somehow compel the Beaverin to break down the bark; it is part of a life cycle we barely understand. To put it in Earth terms, the Beaverin are the slaves of the Treeforms.

The Treeforms didn't like us talking directly to their slaves.

*Punish*, said Thumbs, through the clear curved wall of the envirodome, and gave me a thumbs down.

All creatures who are in any way like humanity have developed the concept of punishment.

The news report, so glib, so sure, so wrong in so many details, comes to a close and a message arrives for me. Framed in polite terms, Group F wonders if I'm available to answer some questions via a netlink? If that wouldn't be an interruption. Apparently the situation on Demeter has developed.

The worse it gets, the more polite the messages seem. This is the frosty edge of diplomacy, and it means I'm in trouble. I could refuse, claim I am not up to the task. But I am overwhelmed with the desire to know—what is really happening there? Is it as bad as they're saying on the lowest paywall? Is it as bad as everyone in the world believes?

If I could only help, get out of this place and find a way
to—

Here come those feelings again. I push them down.

I reply:

Of course. I'm available as from now.

A private multivox opens on the desk. It shows me a room,
I'm guessing within Group F headquarters where I found
my old coin next to a tall white pillar one day. Although
the room is not grand, or white. It's small. Poky, even, with
standard blue walls and no windows. Three people are
sitting around their desk connection, upon which a link to
Demeter has been thrown. A forest planet, much like Earth,
stunning in its blue and green livery, it rotates in speeded-
up time. The faces of the three don't interest me as much as
that beautiful world, but I can't simply stare at it. I have to
pay attention to these faces, and read what I can from the
way they address me.

There are no introductions. The central figure, an older
man with groomed facial hair and a military uniform,
says, 'What, in your opinion, is the best way to attempt
communication with the dominant beings on Demeter?'

Here we go. Public opinion has worked its magic. It had
been quietly suggested during the hearing that we might
withdraw from the situation and allow it to 'work itself out'.
Meaning let the Beaverin be punished, I suppose.

I picture Thumbs, outside the envirodome, giving me the
thumbs down.

But now I have a chance to change things, and I have
just the information that might work. I've been reading
around and formulating this for a few days, and here is the

right moment for it, like a gift. I might just save us both. 'Underground vibrations,' I say. 'That's my best guess. Something through the root systems.'

'Can you elaborate?'

'You could examine the work being done by the Beijing group into tiny low-frequency communications. All sound is vibration, after all.'

The man frowns. 'Have you talked to anybody else about your theory?' The tone is harsh. They are beginning to think of me as not allied to their cause. The way they sit, and the deliberate image of the planet, speeded up. The lines of the shoulders and the mouths. This is the very beginning of distrustful manipulation. Worst case, they'll cut me loose. My career will be over, and I'll be thrown to the lions of public opinion.

Wait. I'm getting ahead of myself. I just need to pull this conversation back and prove my usefulness. Vibration theory could save me. Seeds of discontent can remain dormant; I've defused situations worse than this in trade negotiations before.

'I've only just discovered it. It's a low fund project, but the applications are wide ranging, although they aren't thinking of it as a communication technique. I'd look further into it, but currently much of the data is above my paywall.'

The body language has shifted into interest, possibly relief, even while all the older man says is a statement of guarded encouragement:

'We'll get back to you. Thank you.'

The three faces, the desk, the room, Demeter: they all fade away.

Less than a minute later I receive a message informing me that my paywall status has been upgraded. That's the fastest

I've ever seen Group F move. It reinforces my belief that all the power in that room was held by one person. A person who had already made some decisions about me before we spoke. And it wasn't the man with the moustache.

*Gggri*, says Pipe.

We've started measuring time together. *Gggri* means noon, I think. At least the clock display in the corner of the desk says 12:00, and this is the fifth day in a row Pipe has said the word at that time. We are monitoring the movement of the clock in some kind of harmony, which is an astounding development. But what is more universal than time? Every creature marks it, in one way or another. I've yet to find one who doesn't age. When these six remaining weeks of quarantine are over, both Pipe and I will be older too.

I bring up the Beijing Group's homepage, click on 'Current Projects', and then ask for more detailed information. This time I'm not refused.

*Gggri*, repeats Pipe.

*Noon*, I say. *I get it. But, Pipe, I'm busy right now. Busy. Busy. Busy.*

*Bushy.*

*Busy.*

*Busy.*

Has it understood? It stops talking. It knows about time, and how we use it.

# FOUR
# LIE/TRUTH

A paywall status change means access to a lot more information in many arenas; I wish I could say I wasn't abusing the privilege. At least I didn't make personal searches until after looking further into the Beijing Group's project. I studied their documents and even wrote one of my own, firing it off to Group F with far too much hope attached to it, making it a weighty document for only forty pages. Can I prove my continuing usefulness? I've yet to hear back from them.

Now I've looked at some of the higher grade stuff about me online, I'm surprised they've shown an interest in anything I have to say.

The paywalls are meant to guarantee a better source of document, including academic and politically sensitive information at the highest levels. I used to think the secrets of the universe would be very different from what we were told, but now I see that it all filters down in the end anyway. Some element of the truth informs all. The idea of making a scapegoat out of me started very high up, from what I can tell, and who can blame them? I deserve whatever I get.

But there are others who want to keep ties with me, and nothing personal about me that has leaked into the public domain was manufactured. Not the old lovers with tales of my dominating perversions, or the crews who have claimed I'm distant and cold. It all sounds so much worse in those terms, through other people's eyes.

Who really cares about the past, though? There's a month to go, and by that time I'm sure my youthful failings will be old news. Particularly if I can put forward something else to be remembered for. Such as the Beijing project.

That's going to need a bit of help.

I remove the restrictions on my document, and release it on the lowest paywall setting.

It's noon.

*Shgarg*, says Pipe, which makes me smile.

Lie, I say. *Dop*.

It laughs. *Ghauuuu*. This is our new game. *Shgarg* is evening, as far as I can tell, although it seems to be late afternoon sometimes, and then the stress is on the start of the word.

*Gggri*, says Pipe. Noon.

*Truth*, I tell it. *Pod*. One sound is the elegant reversal of the other. The more I learn of Pipe's language, the more I like it.

We play the truth/lie game for a while. Then Pipe asks me: *Vurgsh?*

*Dop*, I say, and then, after a hesitation, *pod*. I'm good and I'm not. Sometimes there is no difference between opposites.

I can tell Pipe is thinking about this, so I leave it to its thoughts and check online. It's too early yet, of course, but I've become sucked into looking at this digital world. I can't leave it alone, even though whatever is happening on Demeter right now is still above my paywall. But I'm sure that the news will pick up my leak, and then everybody will have an opinion about my involvement in the Beijing project, and what it means for the Beaverin.

Group F will know I put the document out there. Some of them will despise me, but others will, perhaps, admire this move. I'm beginning to understand how this game is played.

Things are good and things are bad.

But I'm still in the game. And I still have a chance to make it right.

# FIVE

# SHUSH

How slowly time can pass when it makes up its mind to do so.

Sometimes I think that the one fact that lies at the heart of me is that I have never had parents.

I've often thought of all the benefits and drawbacks that gives to a person. In a system of tiering and classification my lack of parents put ticks in lots of boxes, as did the fact that I've lived in so many foster homes and learned so many languages. I did not settle anywhere for long; I never felt I'd found my home. But I developed an expert grasp of reading facial expressions and posture. No matter what ethnic or religious group I had been placed in, I learned that people are all the same when it comes to feeling uncomfortable around a child that is not their own. And when you push them to anger—well, that looks pretty much identical everywhere.

The experiment in placing the highest rated children in care with foster parents from a range of backgrounds continues. The public argument is that it fosters diversity, but higher up the paywall talk of 'stretching the comfort zone of future employees in space travel' continues. No long-term attachments formed. Cultivating the ability to dive into any environment and find a way to float.

I know why this is on my mind.

The Campaign for Cultural Childhood—C3—messaged

me this morning to let me know they were thinking of running with a new publicity angle.

C3 is one of the friendlier faces of the system, and I have been part of their literature since my first job. I am one of their success stories, and their online presence tracked me, asked me for quotes. I sold the benefits of my kind of upbringing. Which, to be clear, I do believe in. There were negatives, of course, but if I had been the product of your average household, raised the old-fashioned way, I would not be the person I am today.

I find I can't wish myself different, even with all the mistakes I've made.

It should be the nail in the coffin of my career, this abandonment by C3. But when the expected request for a multivox comes through from Group F, I am prepared. I'm not about to give up.

'Of course, now I'm no longer involved with C3 I'm not tied into maintaining a wholly positive public image,' I tell the usual three faces. 'This could be to everyone's advantage.'

The older man with the moustache, still in the central position, crosses his arms and leans back. He is my enemy. I suspect he may even be behind the initial leaks of my private information, and he is getting impatient to leave me behind because I now also remind him of the fact that he broke the rules. It's a terrible combination of fear and aggression. The way he faces me directly with his eyes glued to my forehead, excluding the others with his rounded shoulders, tells me he's taking this very personally.

This would suggest I'm in trouble, but after a few meetings it has become clear that he's only a figurehead, sitting centre stage, while the real power lies with the woman on his right. And she likes me. She warms to me more each time we speak, and definitely as a reaction to the man's hostility. I'm a lucky pawn in a long-running game between these two players, is my guess.

The angle of her chin has changed accordingly, lowering further with each multivox, almost to the point now of acknowledging an equal. She sees how I'm refusing to be discarded, and she likes it.

And, as befits the middle-man, the creature on the left is from Janus. It's a planet with an amenable government to trade negotiations, and a reliance on slavery of one of the humanoid forms—this information is kept low-key as much as possible, with only occasional flare-ups in the media. I studied them, and was involved in some of the negotiations a few years back. They're usually very hard to read, but this one has been on Earth too long and has started to pick up the mannerisms. It has put its elongated head to one side, its eyes narrowed, and its crest is flat, arranged to fall like human hair. It is evaluating, and open to persuasion either way. Is that even a slight upturn of the mouth, with the sharp teeth of its carnivorous past poking through? What a strange expression on a creature that is informally called, in English, a Pokerface.

'How so?' says the Pokerface, with a sibilant 's' and a clipped 'o' due to its mouth shape. I can't read anything into that.

'You can implement my suggestions regarding vibration communication on Demeter while making it clear that it's my idea.'

'I'd imagine everyone on Earth already knows that,' says the older man, drily, which earns him an eye-flick of disapproval from the woman.

'If the Group was to own it directly, and it failed, it would dent public confidence,' I point out. 'If it's my name on it, then it would be my error, not yours.'

'And if it does work, it's your success, not ours.'

A micro-expression on the woman—a smile.

'Packing a lifeboat for a long voyage is in everyone's best interests,' I say. 'Even the one who accidentally sinks the ship.'

The Pokerface frowns. I've never seen that before. How we all rub off on each other, and lose what is special about us along the way. It doesn't understand the analogy, which is why I used it. There can be no quick decisions now. They must converse about my meanings, my motives, instead of relying on gut reaction. This board has been moving far too quickly for my liking.

'We'll get back to you,' says the man. The multivox ends.

I sit in silence for a while, and then call out.

*Pipe?*

No answer, which is what I expected. But how I hoped otherwise. There's been no communication between us for two days, and the loneliness is hard to bear. The more I stare at the wall, the more I realise that nothing is as important to me at this moment, in this room, as the sound of Pipe's voice.

*Shvas?* I call.

Is it busy? Doing what? Have I offended it? I can't bear the thought. I have said something stupid, something gross and unforgiveable. Something human. Nobody can offend with a single word quite like humanity.

No, it must be busy. Busy is so much better than uninterested. Or gone.

Please don't let Pipe be gone.

It occurs to me that silence—the unnerving quality of it, the loud, shouting voice it gives to the pain of abandonment—

cannot ever be communicated to Pipe. It cannot know how much it is hurting me right now.

I have a new message. The desk flashes, and emits a soft chime, but I can't bear it.

*Shush*, I say. *Ssssshhhhhh.*

This probably means something very different in Pipe's language. It's a deluge of sound; a flood. It's probably the equivalent of a brass band on parade. And yet, to us, it both asks for, and breaks, a long silence.

# SIX

# HERE

*Ash*, says Pipe.

I wake up to the sound of its voice, like waking from a dream to find it's become real. A week has passed; the longest week of my life, and this is not usual human exaggeration. I have never needed anyone before, but I have to accept, in this moment of sudden and intense relief, that I need Pipe. It is a horrible, wonderful feeling.

I know this need is the product of circumstance, but that doesn't help. I'm here. I will continue to be here for another four weeks, and the only creature who can understand what that means is Pipe.

Also, Pipe gives me the most honest conversation I've ever had.

*You're here*, I say. *You're here, you're here, I'm so pleased, I can't tell you.* I struggle to remember any of its language, so strong is the grip of delight. *Vurgsh*, I manage to say. *Vurgsh.*

*Good*, Pipe says.

*Where were you? I was worried about you.*

But, of course, this can't be explained. Except, maybe, the tone of my voice conveys my meaning. If Pipe has started to understand my inflexions as much as my language, there's a chance it understands.

Pipe replies. It's a stream of sound, so beautiful, like water splashing over pebbles. That's when I realise that, in fact, our languages are incompatible. I could never speak Pipe

Language well, because it blends everything together, no beginning or end, no space for breath or pause for thought. Its speech is not a separate function as such. It must cost it a great effort to isolate it into words. How mangled its eloquent language must sound from my mouth.

I listen to it talk, making little sense of it, but through the patterns of the flowing words I glean—what? Relief of its own? Pleasure at being back in my company? I must be putting my own emotions upon it, but I can't help myself.

Eventually, Pipe stops gurgling, and says, *here.*

*Here*, I repeat.

*Wowol.*

*Wowol.* Like an echo in deep water. What does Pipe think *here* means? I'm guessing, *this place.* Or, *being together in this moment.*

We are together in this moment; I don't care if it's an illusion on my part. It has been such a terrible week, in which only work has distracted me from the passing of time. The Beijing project is go, with the catchy social media title of Big Voice. That means we must produce a device that will land, and then bury itself into the soil of Demeter before transmitting our best guess at a peaceful greeting at a depth of a kilometre underground. So much of this project is utter guesswork, hijacking Worm Theory of all things. The Johannesburg Group have been working on a planet with giant earthworms, positing that they must hold high intelligence. With my higher paywall setting I've been able to read it, and commandeer their theories for Big Voice.

I really am about to stake my personal reputation on this mish-mash.

Who am I kidding? I have no personal reputation left anyway. This is all for Thumbs. For if I must admit to myself that I care for Pipe, then it becomes undeniable that I also care for Thumbs.

Thumbs is probably dead. Nearly definitely dead. But I'm still trying to save it, to make myself better than I am. Than the whole world thinks I am.

For I did a stupid thing. I cracked, and asked the desk how many social media messages it was filtering out of my stream in which personal abuse featured, and the answer was—a staggering amount. I'm being held personally accountable for the spreading war on Demeter, as the Treeform aggression decimates the Beaverin population back to whatever it considers to be controllable levels. It's one thing to blame yourself, but another to have the entire world blame you too. And so Big Voice must work. It must.

I find myself explaining it to Pipe, relying on this new sense of connection, unseen and inexplicable. I talk and talk and talk, and I feel that Pipe is listening. What does it matter if individual meanings no longer apply? Communication, in Pipe's world, is a stream. Right now, we are in the stream together.

We are here.

# SEVEN

# SORRY

I wish I could stop looking. But it's the first thing I do every day, when the lights start to simulate sunrise. I search for what the world is saying about me.

I know other things are happening down on Earth. There must be millions of people who know nothing about Demeter or Ottercrash, and wouldn't care if they did. But the constant updates of the news, the way the media machine feeds itself with conjecture and panic, gives me the impression—here, in this small room—that an entire planet is focused upon me and the question of whether I am a good or a bad person.

This question cannot really be answered until Deep Voice is activated. Do I wish, in retrospect, that I hadn't explored my sexuality quite so fully with people who have proved willing to talk about it on social media for the right price? Do I wish I'd behaved better with my myriad of foster parents, and my crewmates? If I do wish it, it's only objectively, as if examining somebody else's life and seeing what would have been a more palatable choice with the bland, easy eyes of the outsider. But when I think about myself, and the things that made me, then I find I would protect every wrong turn on this path; I could not have sacrificed this view, not for an approval rating of one hundred per cent.

Perhaps I'm learning to have a little faith in myself once more.

I once worked on an assessment for a mineral treaty being negotiated between Group C and the dominant species on the planet Diana. They had hunted a number of smaller species to extinction and we offered them rabbits as a suitable replacement: fast breeders, tasty meat, difficult to catch. The deal went ahead, but I advised caution. They had never developed a word for regret. It's difficult to say why that should be. Possibly regret was embedded so deeply within them that they had no need to express it, but their body language suggested, to me, the opposite. I watched footage of them in negotiation and found them charming in manners and interactions, so polite, keen to learn about us. It reminded me of films in which a psychopath takes an interest in a potential victim.

Last I heard, they are enjoying their rabbits. I hope the file is still flagged as dangerous.

In Pipe's world the many kinds of regret that exist are not the same, and this suggests to me that it's a deeply refined culture. If Pipe interrupts me in my long monologues that have become a fixture of our friendship then it starts with a sound like:

*bish*

*Sorry to interrupt*, Pipe says, and then its own monologue starts, and I pick up more sounds I recognise within the flow each time. *Shoush*, for instance, comes up a great deal. But when I think of it, it comes up in my own too. And then there's the juxtaposition of *wowol*.

But back to *sorry*. There's a huge difference between *sorry to interrupt* and *I'm so sorry I wasn't there for you emotionally* that it astounds me to think the English language uses the same word, without even a small alteration. No such confusion occurs in Pipe's language. The types of *sorry* obviously spring from the same root, but have diversified beyond mere inflexion in delivery.

Yesterday, after I received a message to confirm that Deep Voice had landed and buried itself successfully only to trigger a fresh wave of Beaverin deaths in its immediate vicinity, I talked and talked to Pipe. I talked about regret, and I think it's a concept Pipe could have identified with if only I could have found a way to explain it. I talked of love and hate and fear, and loneliness, and what it's like to be chosen by your crew as the one who must communicate what went wrong.

I talked about things I have tried to not even think of since the hearings. The way the Treeforms had grown roots around the Otter, and held fast when we tried to leave the planet. Those roots were so strong; they ripped the underbelly of the ship open. How fast they must have grown, and with such intent. I relive our realisation that we cannot leave, for myself and for Pipe. The discussion about the one-person escape pod, situated on the top of the ship, where the roots had not yet grown. The agreement that I should be the one to go.

Apparently Thumbs reported later through the communications equipment left in the wreckage that the rest of the crew had been killed, the bubble ruptured by root growth, the air compromised. Demeter has richer oxygen, at a higher pressure. Oxygen toxicity would have claimed them. I found this out when my paywall was upgraded. Nobody thought to tell me in person.

I described it all to Pipe, as clearly and as accurately as I could, and then I spoke about arriving here. I needed people after what had happened on Demeter. I needed someone with me beyond the digital, in the interaction that only exists when people sit in the same space and look at each other, and breathe in what has been breathed out by another. And how you, Pipe, how you somehow began to fill that need in me. Even though I don't even know if you have lungs, and we're nowhere near being in the same space in any other way than our mutual desire to understand. But that is enough for me. It's more than enough.

I told you then of what it meant when your voice was absent last week. I still don't understand why you stopped communicating. Or perhaps I couldn't hear you. Either way, the thought of it happening again is the thing I dread most, even more than the activation of Deep Voice tomorrow.

*I missed you, Pipe*, I said. *I missed you.*

And you said—*baaaash.*

I knew what it meant.

It's perfect for Pipe's form of communication, of course. It allows me to understand the nuances of tone that were a mystery to me in our early attempts to speak. Depths and shallows, that's the key, in watery terminology. *Bish* is light, dappled, playful at times. *Bish* is a stream, or perhaps where a calm sea meets a beach. *Baaash* is ocean. *Baaash* can rise up out of the blackness, where strange monsters lurk. It means—I'm sorry. It really means it.

After that I got excited about how to draw out sounds to temper meaning in Pipe's language, but it didn't work with every example. Far from it, in fact. When I drew out *plip* to suggest the interminable nature of our incarceration:

*plaaaap*

I heard *ghauuuu* for quite some time afterwards. I wonder what I said. I think it might have been rude.

The Beaverin said sorry in many different ways. Looking back on it, that should have suggested to me that they weren't top of the food chain. The head of the Catholic faith on Earth—at one point the most powerful person on the planet—couldn't actually be wrong. Papal infallibility, they called it. The higher up you go, the less you need to express regret. Instead you simply rewrite to suit.

So I've been writing my own document to put out there, if Deep Voice fails. A last attempt to save my skin. I've been trying to think of so many ways to say sorry for the blame Group F will heap upon me. It has occurred to me that the word sorry doesn't even sound very apologetic. It's too sibilant, and quick to climb from honest sentiment to sarcasm, even annoyance. I really am truly, completely, undeniably sorry for my mistakes on Demeter, but the more I say it, and the more I pile up adverbs in front of it, the less sincere it sounds.

I have pushed emotion down for too long. For all my guilt and desperation there is a part of me that is not touched by it. A part that wants to survive in spite of everything I've ever done wrong, and I have been sitting in this room for too long.

I have been sitting in this room for too long.

When I read my grovelling document back, I find I want to insert a real word instead. A word I can believe in.

I want to put—*baaash*.

# EIGHT

# PLEASE/ THANK YOU

The more planets we contact that hold sentient, communicating life, the more we realise that languages, so much as species, go to war.

At one singular point in Earth's history, the year 2009, there were 6,909 languages being spoken, and twenty wars being fought. Imagine that year. The glorious, horrible mess of it: everybody shouting, nobody communicating. The wars were won and the winners took what they wanted: resources, people, and the words that suited them. They pillaged each language and concept that appealed. A large language, containing over one million words, will hold so many corpses within it. In the process of ingestion many original meanings will be lost, and new ones will be born.

Five minutes to go.

I sit in the dark. I'm watching a live feed of Deep Voice's systems. It displays its vital functions, like a patient at a hospital. The organic components provide the energy, while the mechanical and digital components do their work. What humanity can accomplish is amazing, now that we're all officially speaking the same language.

The outer hull is about to be compromised; that's why the activation has been brought forward. The casings have moved a quarter of an inch in the last hour. In the field of bio-mechanisation, this is a chasm. It's incredible that the dog's heart within is still beating. We don't know what's causing the breach but in my dream last night I pictured roots, pink and twisting, burrowing through the soil to find my own body trapped within Demeter's core. They coiled around my wrists and ankles, the rough, damp ridges pulling tight, and then worked their way up to my mouth, sliding in, over my tongue, bringing the taste of dirt and death. Down my throat, deep into my lungs, they travelled, until there could be no more words, no more sounds.

I woke up and called for Pipe. I was amazed to find I still had a voice, and that it sounded strong in such darkness. Pipe replied, and soothed me as nobody has before; kind words in the night must be one of the great gifts that parents give to their children. I think my life would have been very different if I had received them for the first time when I was younger, and capable of believing them.

The Treeforms must grow at an exponential rate if they are able to pull apart Deep Voice so quickly. I spoke of my theories on this in the hearings, but I think much of what I said was chalked up to post-traumatic stress, and therefore ignored. Treeform growth and movement appears to have been estimated according to Earth principles. It's an oversight we make a lot—refusing to imagine how different things can be.

The clock on the top left of the desk projection tells me there are four minutes to go.

A written message arrives from Group 7:

> Beaverin 000023 reports no change.
> Standing by to update upon activation.

Short and sweet. The recipients aren't listed, of course, but I wonder who is receiving this message, and whether I've been placed on the list by mistake. I'm not meant to have any further contact with the beings I befriend once I leave a planet, and usually that includes no individual updates about their welfare.

Beaverin 000023 is Thumbs.

Thumbs was the brightest of the initial contact group. As soon as I met it, I knew I could work with it; it had a curiosity about me, and it wanted to try to form English words between its oversized tongue and prominent front teeth. Its own language—in an infancy stage—was similar to many I've come across on forest planets, emulating the natural sounds around it. I've always found these first steps into language beguiling.

Thumbs is still alive. It is a brave creature, in a state of abject starvation by now. It was the one who came to the bubble, alone, and spent frenzied hours trying to explain to me why the Beaverin had begun to die in vast numbers, poisoned by the treebark they had consumed so happily only hours before.

Three minutes to go.

I take advantage of my paywall upgrade and retrieve the footage I filmed of Thumbs outside the clear, curved wall of the bubble. It is not really much like a beaver at all. It reminds me of the pictures I've seen of Neanderthal man, but retaining a waterproof pelt, and the jaw dwarfs the rest of the face. The eyes are still placed on either side of the head, which tapers to a point and bears a tuft that each Beaverin wears in a unique way. Thumbs has a quiff, of all things. I wish I didn't find it so adorable.

It stands upright, too, like a man, and wears a garment of leaves, chewed and shaped into a loose dress by its own saliva. Beaverin saliva is amazing stuff, containing antibiotic and antiseptic properties, and other compounds that we have not yet been able to duplicate on Earth. Antibiotics are big business. Believe it or not, this is what we're trying to set up a trade link for: to get the Beaverin to spit into jars.

Would we be trying to save them from the war we triggered if they didn't have amazing saliva? I don't believe this is a particularly difficult question to answer. But then, humanity cultivates such cynicism for fun. The Beaverin have no such instincts, and so Thumbs is absolutely earnest as it splays its blue webbed fingers on the bubble's surface and tries to overcome its panic to talk to me. Eventually we find mutual meaning—the Beaverin have lied in the hope that they could break free of the Treeforms. They have been leading up to ask for weapons in our negotiations, and the Treeforms have somehow uncovered their intentions, and are deliberately poisoning them.

We are not even close to understanding the relationship between the Beaverin and the Treeforms. Is it a form of telepathy between them? How does the chewing and forming of the bark benefit the Treeforms? How can the bark that sustained the Beaverin suddenly be poisoning them, and why would the Treeforms risk killing so many of their needed slaves in this way? I would have stayed, and tried to find out more, so much more.

*Leave*, Thumbs said, in English. *Go*. It might have said *escape* if we had developed that concept together, but its dreams of freedom had not yet led to the formation of the language to match it. Its oppression meant that it didn't dare to even put its hopes into words.

Two minutes.

'Please,' I say, to nobody, to nothing, to the Earth, to Demeter, to Thumbs. 'Please.'

You could think, I suppose, that Thumbs is as much to blame as I am. Didn't it lie? But then, wouldn't you, if you saw your chance to be free of an ancient oppression? We don't understand the relationship, but it's hard not to cast it in human terms as an abusive one. Or perhaps that's just me, bringing my memories to a world that does not need them.

*You want it?* I have said to my lovers, so many years ago. *I know you do. Tell me you want it. How much?*

I want it, my lovers have told me, and I knew at that moment the words were forgeries, designed to please me, and that made me angry. I was heavy-handed sometimes. I forced these games too far. I told myself it was mutual. I knew it had been born in those endless foster homes where there was no power of my own, no way to make anybody bend to my will. I told myself that made it forgiveable. Now, in black and white all over the world's media, the truth is easier to spot, and I understand that the threads of guilt have always been deep inside me, and I am the abuser. I have always been an abuser.

*Please*, said Thumbs in English. *Go.*

Perhaps it meant—*stay*. It was a good liar. Many creatures are, when telling me things they think I want to hear.

I close down the image of Thumbs outside the bubble, and enlarge the stats of Deep Voice. The heart is wavering; life signs are down.

One minute.

I count. I count down the seconds. I count. I count. I count.

Five.

Four.

Three.

Two.

One.

The vital statistics jump, reaching peaks of activity, and then settle back into a regular rhythm.

I receive a message from Group 7. One word:

Active.

*Please*, I say, louder. *Please*.

It is now transmitting a carefully chosen message. Music, in fact, to start—a scale, then tonic triads. Music is, after all, mathematics. We've always started our communications this way, since Voyager worked its magic and brought the technology of a trading planet to our world, opening up all possibilities.

I wonder what the Treeforms are thinking.

It's too early to know, of course, it's too early to know a thing. We must wait to hear from Thumbs to know what, if any, difference we are making. Thumbs liked hand gestures; it was a form of communication they hadn't developed. They used their stubby tails in incredibly expressive ways, and also their chins and cheeks. Their hands remained curiously inert, clasped together, the arm muscles underdeveloped even though they had opposable thumbs. Thumbs loved 'thumbs up' and 'thumbs down' to express emotion, perhaps because of its novelty value.

*Ash*.

It's Pipe.

*Please*, it says. *Please*.

I don't understand why it is saying that word to me at first, but then I get it—it's repeating me. I've been saying that word so much.

*Please?*

'I need this to go right,' I say. I need, please, for this to go right. Please. This guilt, it's so heavy. It hurts. Please.

*Please*, Pipe repeats, and I can tell it's mystified. Here is a word I can't explain, circumstances I can't elucidate. To other creatures I've taught this concept with the giving and taking of items, putting please and thank you together as mirror images. You take, I give. A useful start for potential trading. But I can't give Pipe a thing, and also I'm not asking it for a favour. This time I'm asking the universe, God, luck and fate for a favour, all at the same time. I'm speaking to everything, and to myself.

No matter what I do, there will be some words and some thoughts that can't be translated. I thought I was getting to know Pipe, but I will never have a clue if it understands the eternal, raw, outward, desperate nature of *please*. Or the immense, soul-soothing balm of relief that comes with *thank you*.

To say *please*, and mean it, is to believe that life itself can be persuaded in your favour.

The life signs of Deep Voice are diminishing. The dog's heart inside is giving up. The message continues to be sent, working its way through the program, until the heart comes to a stop, and the peaks and troughs on the display become a still, straight line.

Deep Voice is dead.

'Please,' I say again. 'Please.'

Pipe replies. It says a phrase it has used in the past:

*Ooohmashababab*

A lyrical, enjoyable phrase to master. I have taken it to mean—I don't understand. Sometimes, when I talk for hours, Pipe says it, and then laughs. This time it doesn't laugh.

A message arrives from Group 7:

> Beaverin 000023 reports a cessation of all Treeform
> underground activity in the immediate vicinity of Deep Voice.

I reply to the message, not caring if I'm breaking protocol:

> Any responding communication/vibration?

*Ooomashababab*, repeats Pipe.
Message from Group 7:

> Beaverin 000023 reports Treeforms dormant. No response.

There is a picture attached to the message. I open it, and laugh aloud. It's Thumbs, all big teeth in a gaunt, starved face, holding up his hands, his opposable thumbs pointing to the sky.

Thumbs up.

'Thank you,' I say. 'Thank you.'

Pipe doesn't understand. Nobody will understand, but it still doesn't matter. I'm grateful to the universe beyond any word but one.

# NINE
# FUTURE

I no longer require three people on my case. I have been made the sole charge of the older woman. The way she looks at me makes me feel like I know her well.

That's how I can tell I'm not going to win this fight. I've persuaded so many creatures to sign up to so many things, and I get the feeling what I'm asking isn't hers to grant.

Still, I have to ask.

'I have a strong working relationship with Beaver in 000023 and that could only be beneficial in such a dangerous time,' I say.

'I'd much rather we put our efforts towards discussing a realistic future,' she says. She's no longer sitting in that small room. I'd guess that she's now projecting from her own office, which is a much grander affair. The desk at which she sits is an old dark wood, and the standing lamp is antique, I'd say—the genuine article. The wall behind her is glass; she sits with her back to it as she addresses me, and I can see yellow hills dotted with sheep, and curved, green houses that blend in. It's one of the high-end gated communities inside its own bubble, keeping out bad air and bad people, generating everything it needs for its own upkeep.

'I can be of use on Demeter.'

'Is this about their plight, or about you?' She pronounces the word plight with stiffness, but then, it's not a word that people usually say. It gets used in articles, mostly. It's a good word to distance readers from reality. 'Everything is in the hands of the microbiologists now. The Paris Unit.'

'They need people,' I point out. 'They're advertising internally now.'

'You're making use of your paywall upgrade, I see. That's not what you're meant to be worrying about. You have many other skills, don't you? Let's utilise some of those instead.'

I swallow. I feel hot and tired. Scratchy inside. 'All life on Demeter will die.'

'It seems melodrama is also one of your talents. That might come in useful in your new post. C3 want to reinstate you. You're a hero. You can continue to represent them as they're scaled down.'

'The programme's being—discontinued?'

'It hasn't been entirely successful,' she says, delicately. Then she swivels in her chair and looks out of her glass wall, at her perfect view. Her hair is white, and coiled up tight at the back of her neck. I wonder why she can't look at me. It's not shame. The curve of her spine suggests defeat, failure. Am I the failure, or is she?

'But public reception ratings have never been higher,' I say.

'That's true.' She turns back to me. 'That's why it will quietly disappear. There are new initiatives in the pipeline.'

So I'm to be a poster child for something that's dying. This seems appropriate. I try to imagine myself saying only what I'm told to say, and when to say it. No doubt none of it will be true.

The woman leans forward. She unclasps her hands, and opens her posture to me. This, finally, is honesty. This is what she wants to say. 'We thank you for two things. You made us look good. And you avoided a catastrophe.'

'But Demeter—'

'No. Forget Demeter. We were going to try Deep Voice technology on the Earthworms, but the evidence now suggests it would have killed every one on the planet, and the production of valuable minerals would have ceased. Now we know better. That's the reason you're being given a nice job with a nice place to live.' She gestures at the wall behind her. Now I understand; I'm not looking at her home, but at mine. I see her inclusion of me in the way the corners of her mouth turn up. A real emotion. 'It's not so bad,' she says. 'I promise.'

Our home, then.

She ends the communication. My throat hurts. My head hurts. In a few weeks I will become a person at a desk, just like her. Meanwhile, Earth celebrates the saving of the Beaverin. The information that Deep Voice has somehow paralysed the Treeforms in its immediate vicinity, and that paralysis is spreading across the planet, will be behind the kind of paywall that only those at the very heart of power can afford. The paralysis has made the bark inedible, and who knows what other damage it's done to the planet. Unless we can find a way to counteract it the Beaverin will continue starving to death anyway.

I failed them. I have to find a way to make it better.

I bring up the homepage of the Paris Unit, and request access to their high-level articles. The words blur on the screen. My head is crawling with pain.

My request is refused. It would seem that my paywall status has been downgraded.

# TEN

# ILL/
# CHANGED

The Doctor tells me I was out of it for two days.

I don't remember much. The white bodysuits of the doctors merged into clouds. There were things in my throat.

*It was the swelling of the throat that worried us most*, the Doctor says. *It was impeding breathing. Also, you were quite determined to try to speak.*

I can't tell if the Doctor finds this amusing or troublesome. The voice is a projection from the suit, English delivered in robotic monotone. Instead of a face, there is a screen that projects a generic smile against a pink background, while the word 'Doctor' scrolls across the bottom in many written languages from across the universe. Apparently I'm no longer in any danger, but still I feel as if I'm the one static point in the centre of a storm of light and sound. A smile on a pink background where a face should be. Is there even anyone inside the suit?

Yes? I croak. My throat is shredded; even through the haze of painkillers I feel it.

*You fought against treatment. You kept saying Pipe.*

I nod.

The room is the same. I was not moved, which would have compromised the facility, of course. But somehow it seems different to me. As if the angles have changed, or maybe it's the quality of the artificial light. Everything is too small, and too bright.

*Probably best to rest the voice now*, says the Doctor, but I can't, I can't. What about Pipe? It must be worried about me. I dreamed of rushing water, tumbling to the rocks, sinking deep into soil to find me locked within, and I can't describe the pleasure as the water washed the dirt from me and I rose up clean.

*If it is from Demeter it's got an unusually long incubation period*, says the Doctor. *It's been marked up on the file. We'll need to do some additional tests once you're stronger. Rest, and we'll check on you later. Probably by remote.*

The white, puffed suit steps back from my bed, and leaves through the door that I nearly forgot existed. Look at that— the door still works. No doubt they've erected an extra bubble on the other side, just to be safe. The Doctor will strip off the suit and emerge, weak and small. The Doctor will be scrubbed and scrubbed until everything is clean and uncontaminated. They think this illness came with me from Demeter, but I have other ideas.

There is a crack between Pipe and I, a crack somewhere in the perfect bubbles of our incompatible lives. Through that crack we found each other, and exchanged things. Thoughts. Words. Organisms. It is changing me. I hope I am not changing it too much, for I love it as it is.

I lie in silence for a while, caught between the desire to call for Pipe and the need to rest my throat. Eventually, Pipe makes the decision for me. It speaks, and I find I have to answer.

Noon, Pipe says, as the clock display on the desk chimes.

*Gggri*, I reply, and, wow, it hurts. Pipe's language is so hard on the vocal chords. *Baash*. I'm sorry I haven't said much. But I am here. *Wowol. Wowol.*

*Vurgsh*, says Pipe, and then there is a long, low stream of communication that I can't begin to follow. I think I make out *vah* at one point, and then it dries to a trickle, and Pipe says *vurgsh* over and over. *Vurgsh.*

I was *ill*, I say. *Ill.* I think it must be able to hear the illness in my voice, thin and cracked, but perhaps that's too much to ask.

*Ill*, Pipe repeats, and then says. *Ashashp. Ashashp.*

*You were ill too. Ashashp*, I say. Pipe? *Ashashp?*

*Ashashp*, Pipe confirms.

I picture Pipe ill, and it hurts. I don't actually want to picture a body at all for my friend, or any kind of mortality. Just a voice that links to a mind. I'm beyond even thinking of a face. Pipe is purely a feeling.

The doctors don't seem to have realised that Pipe was ill. Or perhaps that we've had the same illness. Either way, it's lucky. If they put the symptoms together they'd know there's some sort of breach between our rooms, and then all hell would break loose. Tests, questions, and a move to different surroundings. No more conversations. No more Pipe.

*Stay with me*, I say. The words come from the core of me, from a place that rarely speaks. *Stay.*

A human would be embarrassed by the need in my voice. There would be a reassurance, hardly meant, and then maybe a joke to lighten the mood. That's what a human would do.

*Ashashp*, Pipe says, softly.

Perhaps it's not speaking of illness. Perhaps it's speaking of what the illness has done to us both. We have come through a fever of silent days, and found each other on the far side.

Pipe speaks on and on, and I rest my voice and listen. We have shared this alteration, and I will never speak of it to another. Even if quarantine is breached—even if every other soul in this facility dies from the disease that has slipped

181

through the crack—I will not give up my friend in these last weeks together. I already carry so much guilt that more will not matter now.

# ELEVEN
# FRIENDS

One of the caveats of my new job is that I talk to a psychiatrist on a regular basis, starting immediately. This is to be a monthly event. I suppose I have become so much more important, in the sense that I'm to be in the public eye regularly.

Even with a lower paywall, I can track the mountain of material that references me. It's being produced mainly across social media, where every aspect of my past and my appearance is commented upon. I both started and ended a war. How many people can be a symbol of both the factions that want to limit xenotrade, and the groups who campaign for the establishment of universal agreements? Whether you want an Earth alone or a universe of unity, I'm the image for you.

This kind of responsibility apparently needs a psychiatrist, just so I can fulfil my public appearance schedule. Apparently this is already booked up for the next year upon my release from quarantine. I'd imagine many of my speeches are already written.

I don't mind. I really don't. What use am I otherwise?

My first session is booked for next Tuesday, which will be my second day back on Earth. What a strange concept next Tuesday is, after these timeless weeks. I already know one thing—I will never discuss Pipe. Pipe will belong only to me. Any conversation could only serve to change my feelings about this friendship, particularly once I'm gone from this place. A professional voice of wisdom would say—*you projected your thoughts and feelings on to a creature who could not possibly share them.*

I can't disagree with that, but the truth is that it's all projection. I'll project my own misgivings to the psychiatrist. I've projected my own humanity on to so many creatures. Some things only become a problem when we choose to see them in that light, and I don't want to ever see Pipe as a symptom of my incarceration.

I think a lot about meeting up afterwards. Meeting in a place where air and water can mix—well, if we can't imagine such a place, then what use is imagination at all? I think of travelling to Pipe's home planet one day. But here's the thing that bothers me when my thoughts lead me in that direction; why have I, so well travelled, never heard of a being like Pipe? Then the notion creeps in that maybe I have constructed a treasured companion and a true language out of some dodgy plumbing.

A psychiatrist would find that notion and polish it until it twinkles.

But when I say, in those moments, *Pipe? Pipe? Wowol?*

It replies—*wowolash. Wowolash.*

And this soothes me, and my sanity. No sound has ever reassured me more. In these last days of quarantine, before my new life begins, I find myself saying:

*Pipe. Ash. Friends.*

I whisper it to the wall, in the night, and Pipe says:

*Friends. Ssshhhh. Friends.*

Such sentiments take me back to sleep.

*Ssshhh* is such a simple sound. The basic sound of its language, perhaps—the running of water in its most straightforward form. *Ssshhh* as friendship suggests to me that togetherness, openness, are key concepts in Pipe's world. What a wonderful way to live that must be.

And then I feel such sorrow that Pipe is here, alone, because of the rules of Earth. Earth has everything its own way. It exports itself wholesale. I'm glad I will no longer travel; I don't want to take this pathetic culture any further into the universe. But it has occurred to me that slowly, slowly, through a process of osmosis, alien cultures are beginning to blend into Earth's. Maybe we will become a better society, if they will only be patient with us and our terrible mistakes. But how forgiving can we reasonably expect the universe to be? The Beaverin and the Treeforms can't be the first time everything has gone wrong, and won't be the last. It has all been so expertly hushed up, and here I am—a hero.

Humanity can't change fast enough for me.

I've anthropomorphised it all again. In my version of events, Earth is now a naughty child and the universe is a patient adult. Only Pipe's *ssshhh* soothes my brain.

This morning I awoke from another dream of water, and I lifted my hand to my face and found it coated with droplets that blended together to make a sheen upon my skin. And I realised Pipe might not be alone in this facility after all. Pipe might be one of many, so many. Contained within this place, yes, but within a thousand drops, working, moving together, making for a kinder, better intelligence than one brain alone.

Pipe might not be it. Pipe might be they.

I've been sitting still for far too long. My lunch sits untouched beside my desk; I find I've had less appetite in these past few days, and I cry more easily. I cry at anything.

My emotions must pour out of me, just like sweat. I am becoming a being of water.

*Ash?* says Pipe.

*Wowol, Pipe.*

*Shvas?* it says. Or they say. *Ghauuuuu.*

I laugh back.

The language streams forth, and I catch more and more words I know. *Shoush.* It talks of home, and *shgorg.* Evening. Time and its constraints.

As I listen I search online, looking for any mention of liquid creatures, water language. But my paywall no longer includes access to any scientific material, not even in my own field. How stupid I have been, not to see this coming. To realise that I would only want to find out about Pipe once all this was drawing to a close.

I can find nothing. There's not even a whisper on social media, where usually everything filters down to basic gossip. Pipe continues to talk, but the concepts are far beyond me now, and it all runs together into a great waterfall, growing and growing in volume, so that in the end I am forced to shout:

*Ooohmashababab*

Then it dries to a trickle, and stops. We hold the silence between us, for a while.

*Bish*, says Pipe, and then *ghauuuu.*

I have a new message from Group F:

Beaverin 000023 appointed Earth envoy in response to decision to evacuate key members of Beaverin population to Earth, and your presence requested at negotiations. Your quarantine termination date moved forward under special dispensation. Prepare for immediate return to Earth and commencement of public appearance schedule.

I should have seen this coming too.

The acceptance that Demeter cannot be saved, and the decision to dress it up as an invitation to the Beaverin—well, I thought that might happen. The fact that I'd be expected to attend in order to make it look good did not occur to me. Perhaps I was foolish enough to think I had paid my dues, and I could start to leave my guilt behind.

But it means that I will see Thumbs again, and that brings joy. Yes, I will dare to name this feeling. It's joy. To know that, whatever I did wrong, I did not kill Thumbs, and that I will get to say sorry in person. If sorry means so little, why am I this happy at the thought of saying it?

I start to talk, and Pipe listens.

I talk the blame through, all of it, from beginning to end. The people I repelled, the lovers I misused, the creatures I manipulated, and the lies I told. The decision I now face. I will stand on the world's stage and meet Thumbs again. I will get the chance to help them by finding a way to explain that they should never trust a human being. We are, all of us, beyond redemption.

Thumbs and the Beaverin will get the best deal possible from our world. I will see to it, no matter what it costs me.

If Pipe understands my determination at this moment, it is wise enough not to attempt an answer. There can't be answers any more.

There can only be the comfort of knowing that somebody—somebody that I will never be in a position to hurt—is listening.

# TWELVE

# SAME

Here's the thought that drives me, in our last minutes together: if I get the best deal possible for the Beaverin at these negotiations then it will be at the expense of my employers. I will never regain a position with a higher paywall rating.

I don't care about the house in the gated complex or the high-profile poster campaign. All I want is to win back the right to view top-level material. If I really please the right people, then I might even be allowed to look into quarantine files, and see who shared space with me.

I might be able to track down Pipe.

Thumbs or Pipe? Try to repair my mistakes of the past, or attempt to find a new future? I cannot make this decision.

Here's how we finally communicated that our time together was up:

*Gggrii dop*

*Sugarg dop*

*Baash gggrii sugarg*

To translate: *Noon and evening are lies, and I am so sorry to say it.*

It is a poem of a thought.

The clock in the corner of the desk display says 7:56 am quarantine time, and there is nothing to be packed. I'm naked—following exit instructions. All the clothes I have worn here will remain. Nothing leaves this place but my body, cleaned and checked and ready to return. Four minutes until the door will open. My palms are wet; I rub them on my knees. They are wet too.

What will I do?

*We will meet again*, I say. *Future.*

*Ash*, says Pipe. My name is so close to the word for *friend* in its language. What a wonderful gift that is. I will forever think of myself as a friend, and that will help me to be kinder, when the endless guilt and shame threatens to swamp me.

I will use the memory of Pipe to remind myself that I have been damaged as much as I have damaged others, and this is not a special thing. It's just the way my world works. It's been easy to believe, in this room for three months, that I have been at the centre of amazing events. But I'm a tiny part of the intricacies and engineerings of Earth. And I'm not half as clever as I once thought I was. Just as Pipe might be one of so many, I am a drop in the ocean of humanity. We move, we surge, we dash and we flow, and we think that our furious beating upon the far shores of the universe means we are powerful. But we are only the crest of an uncontrollable surge in the tide. Those who rush up from behind to replace me will be just as guilty, and as innocent, as I am. We all have no real idea of where we go, and what we do.

7:59 am.

What if I help Thumbs, and hope Pipe will track me down instead?

It will need to know what to look for.

*Pipe*, I say, *I'm—*

How can I describe myself in words it will understand? There are so many concepts that we haven't touched, and that wouldn't explain it adequately if I said:

I am a gender.

I am an age.

I am a race.

I am an appearance.

I am a sexual preference.

I am so many arms, and so many legs.

I am a head, and I am hair.

I am distinguishing marks.

I am parts that are there, and parts that are missing.

I am a political persuasion, and a collection of opinions.

I am likes and dislikes.

I am a past, and I am a future.

In a world of so many beings, these descriptions only serve the purpose of telling others how I fit amongst them. How I can be separated, and picked out from the crowd. They matter only when I'm amongst others who are so similar in form and function that we are all desperate to find the delineations. This did not matter with Pipe.

I find I do not want it to matter now.

*Same*, I say. *Pipe. Ash. Same. Ssshhhh.*

*Same*, repeats Pipe. Perhaps this is a concept for which it needs no words. If everything is joined, within one body, why would you need to express an opposition to otherness?

8:00 am. The artificial daylight is strong.

The door opens. Beyond it I can see a clean white corridor.

The Beaverin need me, and I will not let them down this time.

Pipe groans. I realise it is saying my name, drawing it out into long, strong emotion. It sounds like falling into a pool of the deepest water. My body prickles with sweat. I am water, and I will take Pipe with me. Pipe is in me, will be with me now, and will find me again.

# GLOSSARY

| | |
|---:|:---|
| Ash | *Pipe* |
| Home | *Shoush* |
| Good | *Vurgsh* |
| Food | *Paps* |
| Long/Bored | *Vah* |
| Pause | *Plip* |
| Busy | *Shvas* |
| Noon | *Gggrii* |
| Lie | *Dop* |
| Truth | *Pod* |
| Evening | *Shgarg* |
| Here | *Wowol* |
| Sorry (shallow) | *Bish* |
| Sorry (deep) | *Baash* |
| I don't understand | *Ooohmashababab* |
| Ill/Changed | *Ashashp* |
| Friends | *Ssshhh* |
| Laughter | *Ghauuu* |

ABOUT THE AUTHOR

Aliya Whiteley is the author of the novels *The Beauty*, *The Arrival of Missives*, *Skein Island*, *Light Reading*, *Three Things About Me*, *Mean Mode Median*, and a collection of short stories called *Witchcraft in the Harem*. She has had almost one hundred short stories published in various anthologies and publications including *The Guardian*, *Interzone*, *Black Static*, and *Strange Horizons*. She has been nominated for the Pushcart Prize twice, and won the Drabblecast People's Choice Award. *The Arrival of Missives* has been shortlisted for the BSFA award for Best Short Fiction and longlisted for the James Tiptree Jr Award.

For more fantastic fiction, author events, exclusive
excerpts, competitions, limited editions and more

VISIT OUR WEBSITE
**titanbooks.com**

LIKE US ON FACEBOOK
**facebook.com/titanbooks**

FOLLOW US ON TWITTER
**@TitanBooks**

EMAIL US
**readerfeedback@titanemail.com**